MANDIE®
AND THE
TORNADO!

Mandie® Mysteries

MANDIE®
AND THE
TORNADO!

Lois Gladys Leppard

BETHANY HOUSE PUBLISHERS
MINNEAPOLIS, MINNESOTA 55438

Mandie and the Tornado
Copyright © 2001
Lois Gladys Leppard

MANDIE® and SNOWBALL® are registered trademarks
of Lois Gladys Leppard.

Cover illustration by Chris Wold Dyrud
Cover design by Eric Walljasper

Published by Bethany House Publishers
A Ministry of Bethany Fellowship International
11400 Hampshire Avenue South
Bloomington, Minnesota 55438
www.bethanyhouse.com

Printed in the United States of America by
Bethany Press International,
Bloomington, Minnesota 55438

ISBN 1-55661-675-9

For
MOLLIE HARDAWAY

May a
star-studded future
await you

and
congratulations to
CECILY MILLEN
for
winning the MANDIE Auction!

About the Author

LOIS GLADYS LEPPARD worked in Federal Intelligence for thirteen years in various countries around the world. She now makes her home in South Carolina.

The stories of her mother's childhood as an orphan in western North Carolina are the basis for many of the incidents incorporated in this series.

Visit with Mandie at *www.Mandie.com*

Contents

"If I can stop one heart from breaking,
I shall not live in vain;
If I can ease one life the aching,
Or cool one pain,
Or help one fainting robin
Unto his nest again,
I shall not live in vain."

—Emily Dickinson,
POEMS I (1830–1886)

Chapter 1 / Away We Go!

Spring holidays had finally arrived in 1903. Mandie was happy as a lark as she went about preparations to go home for the two-week vacation. Her curtailed social agenda was over, because she had somehow managed to stay out of daring escapades since her involvement in the dangers of the dark alley back in October. The winter had been miserable—cold and snowy with very little sunshine. But now the days were bright and warm and longer. The daffodils were peeping through their soil, and the robins had returned. Everything was wonderful.

And Joe Woodard was coming home!

"Oh, spring has come to town today," Mandie sang as she pulled clothes down from the wardrobe to pack in her valise.

"And the birds are singing their say," Celia picked up on the song. Her things were already downstairs waiting for Aunt Rebecca to finish her business with Miss Prudence, after which Celia and her aunt would be taking the train home to Richmond.

"The wind is warm, the day is bright," Mandie sang on.

"My spirit's soaring like a kite," Celia added.

The Misses Heathwood's School for Girls in

Asheville, North Carolina, was closing its doors for the spring vacation. Mandie Shaw was going to run head on into mysteries elsewhere.

Mandie snapped her valise shut and stood up to look at her friend. "You know, Celia, I'm anxious to find out what Uncle John was talking about in his letter—that there seemed to be a mystery about the new folks who've moved into the old house down by the creek."

"Oh, Mandie, he only meant that no one in town seemed to know the people," Celia reminded her.

"But that's what I'm talking about. New people don't just move into Franklin from parts unknown, not knowing anyone. Franklin is so small everyone has always known everyone else's business," Mandie explained. "I wonder what those people do for a living."

Celia smiled and said, "I'm sure you'll find out. Meanwhile, I think we should get downstairs."

"Yes. Come on, Snowball," Mandie replied, stooping to pick up her white cat and fasten on his red leash.

When the girls got downstairs, they found Aunt Rebecca ready to leave and Ben, the driver for Mandie's grandmother, waiting to pick up Mandie's luggage. She was going to Mrs. Taft's house, then her grandmother would be going home with Mandie on the train.

"It's all sitting inside the door of our room, Ben," Mandie told the driver. "I have three bags, so you might want to ask Uncle Cal to help bring them down."

"I can manage, missy," Ben told her with a smile as he started toward the staircase.

Uncle Cal had just come in the front door after carrying out some other girl's luggage and heard the conversation. "I'll go with you, Ben," he said. He followed the driver up the stairs.

"We'll see you on Friday, Mandie," Celia told her as she and her aunt prepared to leave.

"Yes, dear, tell your mother we'll be there," Aunt Rebecca added.

Mandie reached to hug the little lady and said, "Just don't forget."

Mandie threw a kiss as they entered the waiting rig in the driveway to take them to the depot. Celia waved back.

Ben and Uncle Cal, the school maintenance man, came down with Mandie's luggage and put it in her grandmother's rig, and Mandie stepped inside the vehicle.

"See you in two weeks, Uncle Cal," Mandie told the old man.

As Uncle Cal waved, Ben drove the rig down the driveway.

"Ben, have you ever been back through that dark alley again?" Mandie asked as he steered the rig down the road.

Ben looked back at her in surprise and replied, "Now, you know, missy, I ain't been back in dat place. Why, Miz Taft would send me packin' if I dun such a thing and I ain't got nowhere to pack off to."

Mandie laughed and said, "I was just checking. I haven't seen much of you since Miss Prudence and Miss Hope allowed Celia and me to come back to live in the school. And let me tell you one thing, that was the worst part of the punishment for exploring that alley, having to live with Grandmother, right under her thumb, and going back and forth to school and nowhere else for all those months."

"Now, missy, not many months," Ben replied. "I recollect y'all only had to do dat till right after New

Year's, and den you moved back in de school."

"I know, but days can seem like months living under Grandmother's supervision," Mandie said with a big sigh.

"Guess you gwine hafta spend more time wid huh now dat she be gwine home wid you," Ben reminded her.

"Not really," Mandie said, smiling. "You see, my mother and Uncle John will be there. And you can't imagine how glad I am that my mother married my uncle John after I lost my father. Grandmother is afraid of him, so she is not all that strict and bossy when we're at my house."

"Well, here we is," Ben announced as he turned the rig into Mrs. Taft's long driveway and brought it to a halt at the front door of the mansion.

Mrs. Taft was waiting for them. She opened the front door and called, "Ben, leave Amanda's things in the rig and come and get mine. We don't have much time before we have to get to the depot."

"So we are leaving today, then, after all," Mandie said as she stepped down from the rig, holding on to Snowball, and joined her grandmother at the front door.

"Yes, I was able to get the Mannings to take Hilda to their house this morning. They came back from their trip earlier than expected," Mrs. Taft explained. "Come on in, Amanda."

Hilda was the young girl Mandie and Celia had found hiding in the attic of their school a long time ago, and Mrs. Taft had given Hilda a home. But Hilda would not, or could not, speak to anyone. However, she did get along with the Mannings' young daughter and usually stayed with them when Mrs. Taft was away.

"I'm glad we can leave today," Mandie remarked

as she entered the front door and joined her grandmother in the parlor off the hallway. "Holidays always seem so short." She set Snowball down and removed his leash. He ran out of the room.

"Amanda, don't you think you ought to leave that cat here? He may be a lot of trouble on the train," Mrs. Taft said as she sat down.

"Oh no, Grandmother," Mandie quickly replied as she sat near her grandmother. "Snowball won't be any trouble on the train. He usually sleeps the whole trip. Besides, I'm afraid he might get out while we're gone and get lost."

"Ella and Annie will both be here the whole time," Mrs. Taft reminded her.

Ella, the maid, came to the doorway at that moment and said, "Everything's ready, Miz Taft."

"Thank you, Ella," Mrs. Taft replied, rising. "Come on, Amanda, we'll have a little bite to eat before we get that train."

Mandie noticed that it was not a "little bite to eat" but what looked like an entire meal on the table. "Grandmother, I have to tell you I'm not very hungry. It's almost two hours before the noon meal at the school." She pulled out a chair from the table and sat down as her grandmother took her place.

"I know, but if we eat now we won't have to have anything when we get to your mother's house, because they will have already had their dinner," Mrs. Taft replied. "Now, what are you planning to do while you're home?" She passed a platter of ham to Mandie.

Mandie took the platter, removed a very small slice, and laid it on her plate. She was slow in replying because she didn't want her grandmother to know everything. Mrs. Taft had a way of trying to change other people's plans. "Well," Mandie finally replied, "Celia and her aunt Rebecca and Celia's mother are all coming to visit this weekend."

"That's wonderful, dear," Mrs. Taft said, helping herself to the hot biscuits and passing the platter to Mandie. "We'll have to do something special for them, won't we? Let's see, now. We should plan a dinner one night and invite some of your mother's friends."

"But, Grandmother, some of my other friends may be coming, too," Mandie told her, laying down her fork.

"Fine, then we'll just have a large dinner party," Mrs. Taft replied.

Mandie quickly decided it was time to change the subject. She cleared her throat and took a sip of coffee. "Grandmother, did you hear about the new people who have moved into the old house down by the creek? Did Uncle John write and tell you about them, too?" she asked.

Mrs. Taft frowned and said, "Yes, John did mention that in a letter this week. It seems no one knows them or knows where they came from, which is rather strange."

"Uncle John didn't say in the letter to me whether it was a family, whether they had children, or what kind of people they are—old, young, or what." Mandie told her.

"Neither did he give that kind of information when he wrote to me," Mrs. Taft said. "That's probably because no one knows for sure." She sipped her coffee and then added, "Now, to get back to our discussion of the dinner party. Do you know yet whether Joe is coming home for the holidays? Dr. and Mrs. Woodard should be invited to this dinner and of course Joe, too, if he will be out of school."

Mandie closed her eyes and secretly sighed.

Sometimes it was just impossible to change the subject with her grandmother. Then, looking across the table, she replied, "Yes, ma'am, Grandmother. Joe is going home for the holidays, and his vacation just happened to come at the same time our school's did. He wrote that he would see me, but I don't know whether he is coming to our house or we are going to his."

"Well, then," Mrs. Taft quickly said, "I'll get word to Dr. and Mrs. Woodard that we are expecting them at your house in Franklin, along with Joe, of course."

Ella came to the doorway and announced, "It be time to leave, Miz Taft. You told me to let you know when. Ben has the rig waitin' at de door, and dat white cat he be fed and waitin' in de kitchen."

"Thank you, Ella," Mrs. Taft said, rising from the table. "Please tell Ben we will be right there. Amanda, get that cat if you insist on taking him."

"Yessum," Ella replied and went down the hallway.

"Yes, ma'am," Mandie said as she quickly pushed back her chair and went to the kitchen to get Snowball.

Mrs. Taft was never late for anything and had planned this ride to the depot to coincide with the arrival of the train.

Luckily the train was on time and they could get right on board. Mandie had carried one small bag with her, mainly to set on the floor for Snowball to lie on and sleep. She breathed a sigh of relief when the cat seemed to know what her plans were. He curled up on top of it and went to sleep as soon as the train left the station.

Mrs. Taft leaned back in her seat and closed her eyes. Mandie was too excited thinking about going home to sleep. She had not been home since Christmas, and Joe Woodard and his parents had visited for only one day during those holidays. He was still working full time on his studies at the college in New Orleans. And this time he had not said in his letter how long he would be out of school. Time passed quickly while Mandie was deep in thought.

As the train slowed down and came to a halt, Mandie saw her uncle's caretaker, Jason Bond, evidently waiting to pick them up. She reached down and moved Snowball in order to pick up her bag. He stretched at the end of his leash and look up at her sleepily.

"You can go back to sleep as soon as we get to the house, Snowball," Mandie told him.

Mrs. Taft straightened her hat and stood up. "I must have dozed off there," she said, smiling at Mandie.

"Yes, ma'am," Mandie agreed. She followed her grandmother to the door as Snowball walked ahead on his leash.

Mr. Bond greeted them as they stepped off the train. "Howdy, ma'am," he said to Mrs. Taft, and turning to Mandie he added, "Glad you're home, missy."

"I'm glad to be home," Mandie quickly replied and smiled.

"Yes, and I'm glad that jolting train ride is over," Mrs. Taft said.

"Mr. John's rig is right over here, if y'all will just get in, and I'll get the baggage as soon as they unload it," Mr. Bond explained. He led them to the vehicle and helped Mrs. Taft get inside. Mandie followed.

While Mr. Bond was busy getting their luggage, Mandie watched the crowd to see if there was anyone strange who might be one of the new people in the old house. But everyone seemed to be somebody whose name she at least knew.

When they arrived at the house, Mandie's mother, Elizabeth, was there to greet them. "John had an errand to do," she told her mother and Mandie as they settled down in the parlor. "He'll be back soon. I'm so glad you could come, Mother." Everyone hugged everyone. Snowball ran down the hall.

"I couldn't very well allow Amanda to ride the train alone, so I had to come," Mrs. Taft told her daughter.

"And I appreciate that, Mother," Elizabeth said. Turning to Mandie she said, "I suppose the Hamiltons are still coming next weekend."

"Oh yes, ma'am," Mandie said with a big smile. "Celia's mother and her aunt Rebecca will both be coming with her." Pausing for a second, she asked, "Who else is coming to visit while we're here?"

Elizabeth looked at her and said, "Of course Dr. and Mrs. Woodard will be coming, and when Dr. Woodard stopped by last week, he said they expected Joe to be home and that he would come with them."

Mandie smiled and said, "Joe wrote me that he was going home for the holidays. I'm glad they are all coming here." She quickly stood up and added, "I've got to go back to the kitchen to see Aunt Lou and the others."

"Yes, dear, you do that. They are all busy getting the meal ready," her mother explained.

Mandie hurried down the hallway and opened the kitchen door. Aunt Lou turned and saw her and rushed across the room to embrace her. "And how's my chile?" the old woman asked.

"Fine, Aunt Lou. I hope you are, too," Mandie

said, hugging her back. Turning, she greeted all the others. "Liza, Jenny, and Abraham, I'm so glad to see all of you. That's the best part of coming home, getting to see everyone."

"It sho' is," Aunt Lou agreed as she turned back to the pots on the big iron cookstove.

"We's gittin' mo' people in dis heah town," Liza, the young maid, told Mandie. "Somebody dun moved into dat old barn down by de creek."

Mandie immediately turned to look at the girl. "So I heard," she said. "Does anyone know who they are?"

All the servants shook their heads. "Nope, don't nobody know 'em," Liza said, and then with a big grin, she added, "But we plannin' on findin' out, we is."

"How many people are living in that house? Is it a family or what?" Mandie asked.

Aunt Lou turned to shake her head and said, "Dat we don't be knowin'."

"What kind of people have been seen down at the house, then?" Mandie asked.

"Ain't seen nobody, but de light shows in de house at night so somebody's in dere," Abraham explained.

"But dey gwine come out sometime and den we see 'em," Jenny added.

Looking at Aunt Lou, Mandie asked, "That house is not on Uncle John's property, is it?"

"No, my chile, it be jes' right next to de edge of Mistuh John's land," the woman replied. "Had it been on Mistuh John's property, he woulda been down dere lookin' to see who moved in."

Turning to Liza, Mandie asked, "When you get done with your work, do you want to walk down that way with me? Maybe we'll see somebody, Liza."

"I sho' will, missy," Liza replied, grinning. "I been already tryin' to see but ain't seed nuthin' yet."

"I knowed my chile would be 'vestigatin'," Aunt Lou said with a big smile.

Mandie returned to the parlor to wait for Uncle John's return. She wanted to ask him some questions. Maybe he knew more about it than the servants. But one thing was sure—she just had to figure out the mystery.

Chapter 2 / The Light

Not long after Mandie returned to the parlor, Liza came to the door and silently motioned for her to come out into the hall. Mandie glanced at her mother and grandmother, who were deep in conversation about a dinner party for the next weekend. They didn't even notice when Mandie left the room.

"Can you go now?" Mandie quickly asked Liza.

"Sho' can," Liza replied with a big grin as she danced around the wide hallway. "Aunt Lou, she say thirty minutes, dat's all, and den be back to de kitchen to finish he'pin' wid suppuh."

"Then let's get going," Mandie said with a smile as she walked toward the front door and opened it.

"Yeh, let's git on de way," Liza agreed, following Mandie outside.

Mandie stopped to look around the yard and asked, "Liza, what's the best way to get to that old house from here? I don't remember exactly where it is."

"I knows, Missy 'Manda," Liza replied, leading the way to the side of the house. "We goes dis way and it ain't fah." She danced on around the house and turned into a narrow pathway down the hill. Liza never seemed to walk; she always floated.

"Can we get there and back in the thirty minutes

Aunt Lou has allowed you?" Mandie asked as she hurried along behind the girl.

"Sho' can if we don't be foolin' 'round," Liza replied as Mandie caught up to walk beside her. "Ain't no piece, really. I bin checkin' up on dat house evuh since Mistuh John say he saw a light in it t'other night. But I ain't been able to git out aftuh dahk, so I ain't seed de light whut he say he saw down dere. Aunt Lou, she say no prowlin' round aftuh dahk, but mebbe now you got heah I go wid you aftuh dahk when you goes to see de light."

Mandie smiled at her friend and said, "Liza, I'm not sure I can go to look for the light after dark, either. I don't want to get in trouble with my mother while I'm here, and she might not like the idea of me going out after dark all the way down to that house." She hurried on to keep up with Liza.

"Ah now, Miz 'Lizbeth, she nice lady," Liza said. "I don't think she'd mind if we went together aftuh dahk. I looks out fo' you and you looks out fo' me." She suddenly paused and pointed ahead as she said, "Dere's dat house, you see? Ain't much of a house. Looks like a barn to me, don't you think?"

Mandie stopped to look in the direction Liza was pointing. In the distance she could see a small, unpainted, weather-beaten building leaning slightly to the right, with the shutters closed over the one window in view. Spring vegetation had started growing up around it, and the trees under which it stood had fresh green leaves sprouting.

"It's all closed up," Mandie remarked. "How can anyone see a light inside it?"

"Oh, Missy 'Manda, dat house be full of cracks, and de light shine through dem cracks at night," Liza explained. "Leastways dat's whut Mistuh John say."

Mandie glanced around the place where they stood. "Are we still on Uncle John's property, Liza?"

"Yep, right down to dat briar patch yonder. Dat makes de line," Liza replied, pointing down the incline to a thick mass of bushes. "Aunt Lou, she tell me don't go over de line."

"Who owns that property, Liza?" Mandie asked as they continued standing there looking down on the house.

"Mistuh John, he say de man whut lived in dat house left town long time ago, ain't been seed nor heerd of since den," Liza replied.

"I suppose we'd better stay inside our line, but let's walk down right to the property line where we can see better," Mandie said, walking down the hill.

There was not much more to see at the line. Mandie saw the creek that ran on the other side of the old house and could tell the building itself was small, probably one or two rooms, with one shaky-looking chimney running up the back side. The post holding up the corner of the roof over the small porch was leaning, and the porch floor was half gone, rotted away and fallen in.

Squinting to see if anyone was in the bushes around the house, Mandie said, "I don't see anyone. Considering the condition of that old house, I don't believe anyone could be living in it." She held her hand up to shade her eyes as she stared at the structure.

Liza, finally standing still at Mandie's side, also gazed at the house and said, "Mistuh John, he think somebody livin' in dere 'cause he see de light at night. Somebody bound to be makin' dat light, Missy 'Manda, unless a ghost be livin' in dere." Quickly looking at Mandie, she asked, "Whut you think? A ghost, mebbe?"

Mandie smiled at her and said, "No, Liza, I don't think there's a ghost in that old house. Some human being is making the light that Uncle John has seen."

"Den we gwine find dat human bein'? Is dat whut we plannin' on doin'?" Liza replied.

"I'll have to figure out what we can do about solving this mystery," Mandie told her. "I need to talk to Uncle John." She turned to go back up the hill.

Liza, following, said, "Everybody done seed dat light—Aunt Lou, Jenny, Abraham, Mistuh Bond, and Mistuh John. Dat light is dere at night, and now me and you come look at it aftuh dahk, won't we?"

"I'll let you know," Mandie promised.

"We go tonight?" Liza asked, hurrying along behind Mandie.

"I want to talk to Uncle John, and I'll let you know later when we'll go look after dark, Liza," Mandie promised.

When they got back to the house, Liza had to go back to her duties in the kitchen, and Mandie returned to the parlor. She was glad to see her Uncle John had returned and was sitting there with her mother and grandmother.

"And how's my little blue eyes?" John Shaw asked, rising to put an arm around Mandie's shoulders.

"Fine, Uncle John, and already picking up the scent of a new mystery," Mandie replied with a big grin as he took the chair next to hers and they sat down.

"And I have an idea of what mystery that is," John Shaw replied, grinning at her. "Well, so far I haven't been able to figure it out, but there is a light in that old house down there at night, and during the day there is no sign of anyone. I figure someone must have moved in there, but I don't understand why I haven't seen anyone around the place."

"Does the light burn all night?" Mandie asked.

John Shaw laughed and replied, "I have no idea. I'm certainly not going to camp out down there all night and watch. However, I have knocked on the door and there is no answer, no sound whatsoever from inside."

"Have you tried opening the door?" Mandie asked.

"Of course not, Amanda," John Shaw told her. "There could be some unsavory characters shacked up in there, and it could be dangerous to just barge in."

"I suppose I could sit on the hill above it all day and watch," Mandie suggested. "Someone might go in or out and I'd see them."

John Shaw laughed again and said, "That sounds like a waste of time to me. If whoever is in there doesn't want to be seen, they'd never come out with you sitting there watching for them."

"I could sit behind a bush where they couldn't see me," Mandie explained.

"I wouldn't waste my time with it. Sooner or later we'll find out who is in the house," John Shaw told her. "Aren't your friends coming to visit during the holidays? I'm sure you could find better things to do with them."

"Yes, sir, Celia and her mother and her aunt Rebecca are coming," Mandie replied.

"Are they bringing that little Irish orphan that lives with them?" John Shaw asked, smiling.

Mandie grinned back. "Not this time," she said. "They're leaving her with some friends who have a little girl about Mollie's age."

"And your mother said the Woodards are

coming, too," John Shaw said.

"Yes, sir, and Joe, too," Mandie told him with a big smile. "Maybe Joe will help me watch that old house."

"That's not a very interesting way to spend your holidays," John Shaw said.

"We won't just sit there every minute watching. We'll find other things to do," Mandie said, still smiling.

After supper that night, everyone gathered in the parlor, where a fire burned in the fireplace. The days were warm now, but the nights in the North Carolina mountains were still chilly.

The adults' conversation was boring to Mandie as she sat there thinking about the light in the old house. It was dark now, and she desperately wanted to go watch the house for a light. But she was also trying to stay out of trouble, so she didn't dare.

Suddenly she was aware of Liza outside the door in the hallway making signs to her. The girl was waving her hands around and pointing to the front door. Mandie instantly understood that Liza wanted to go watch for the light in the old house.

Mandie hesitated for a moment and then decided not to go running off in the darkness with Liza without permission. She took a deep breath, looked at John Shaw, who was sitting near her, and asked in a low voice that her mother and her grandmother would not hear, "Would it be all right if Liza and I go down and watch the old house a little while? Please, Uncle John?" Mandie smiled at him, her blue eyes shining.

"You are asking permission? I don't believe it," Uncle John teased. "Well, since you asked, I suppose it would be all right if the two of you walked down that way for a little while, but don't be gone too long."

"Thank you, Uncle John," Mandie excitedly replied as she stood up and hurried for the door.

Mandie was proud of herself for actually asking permission to do something instead of barging headlong into it. She had been really trying to behave better since her experience in the dark alley last October.

She snatched her mother's shawl from the hall tree and joined Liza, who was wearing a jacket.

"Uncle John gave us permission to go down there, provided we are not gone too long," Mandie told her friend.

"Right glad he did 'cause I didn't axe, and if Aunt Lou ketch up wid me I jes' tell huh Mistuh John, he say we can go," Liza replied with a big grin as they went out the front door.

Mandie giggled and said, "Liza, I'm afraid you are learning bad ways from me."

The two hurried down the hill to the place where they had stopped that afternoon, and there they sat down on a huge rock where they could watch the house.

"I think we need to be quiet now so no one will know we are here," Mandie cautioned the girl. "But if you see a light, whisper in my ear to let me know, and I'll do the same."

"All right," Liza whispered back.

The moon was shining, but with so many trees between them and the old house, the moonlight was shut out and everything was in darkness. Mandie kept squinting to see the house. She didn't think she would be able to see anyone down there, and she made a quick decision.

She whispered to Liza as she stood up, "Come

on, let's get closer. I can't see a thing from here. Be real quiet."

Liza rose and followed her as she moved down the hill. They crossed the property line, carefully picking their way through the thick bushes. When they were within a hundred feet of the old house, Mandie put out her hand to stop Liza.

"Let's stay right here," she whispered as she found a rocky clearing where they could sit.

The house was in plain view now, and they watched for a light or for anyone going in or out. They waited for what Mandie thought must have been at least an hour, but nothing happened. Reluctantly she decided they'd better go back.

"Come on, Liza, we'd better get back to the house," Mandie whispered to the girl as she stood up.

"But we ain't seed nuthin' yet, Missy 'Manda," Liza protested as she rose.

"But we might wait all night and not see anything. We'll just have to come back again," Mandie told her as she started up the hill.

Liza slowly followed her. "Soon as we leaves, dat light gwine come on," she mumbled.

They climbed all the way to the top of the hill, then paused to look back down at the house. Suddenly there was a faint flicker of light inside it.

"A light!" Mandie said excitedly, pointing toward it.

"I dun tole you," Liza replied.

"Let's go back down the hill, but be extra careful about being quiet," Mandie told her as they started back down the incline.

Suddenly from out of the darkness, Snowball came running down to his mistress. When Mandie bent to catch him, he dodged her and kept right on going.

"Oh, Snowball!" Mandie said in a whisper, hurrying down in an effort to catch up with the cat.

But Snowball headed straight for the old house, jumped up on the porch, and in the darkness knocked over something that sounded like a metal bucket, making a loud noise. The light inside the house immediately went out.

Mandie froze in her steps. Snowball had ruined everything. There was bound to be someone inside the house to put out the light so suddenly.

"Dat cat!" Liza exclaimed in a whisper.

"Yes, that cat!" Mandie agreed, still standing there watching the porch. Snowball was smelling around on it and then decided to jump off and disappear in the darkness.

Mandie slowly and quietly moved down the hill. Liza followed. Finally she spotted the white cat under the house, sitting there washing his face. Quietly stepping up to the house, she bent and tried to get the cat to come out. He just looked at her and continued washing his face. She was afraid to call him, because then whoever was inside would hear her.

Looking about the yard, Mandie found a long stick, which she picked up and went to stoop down and poke at Snowball under the house. The cat made a loud growl of protest and came running out the other side. Liza captured him and handed him over to Mandie.

The girls rushed up the hill and stopped at the property line to look back. There was no sign of a light.

"We'll come back tomorrow," Mandie told Liza. "And I'll be sure Snowball is shut up somewhere."

"Dat white cat sho' ruint it all," Liza declared.

They walked up the hill toward the Shaws' house.

"There's definitely someone in that old house," Mandie said, holding on to Snowball as she walked.

"Sho' is, so whut we gwine do 'bout it?" Liza asked.

"I'll have to think about it," Mandie said.

"When all dem friends of yourn comes, dey kin he'p us, can't dey?" Liza asked.

"They won't be here till the weekend. I hope we have this mystery solved before then," Mandie replied.

"Dat we kin do, jes' you and me," Liza agreed.

"We'll just keep watching. Whoever is in there has to come out sometime for something," Mandie declared.

They reached the yard of John Shaw's house, and Mandie looked back but the old house was out of sight.

She hoped when whoever it was came out she would see the person. She would have to more or less camp out within sight of the old house. And if no one ever came out when she was watching, why, maybe she would get up the nerve to just go knock on the door.

Chapter 3 / Spying

Mandie didn't see Uncle John until the next morning. He had gone up to his office to do some bookwork before she and Liza came back. And her mother and grandmother were still planning the dinner party, so she didn't mention going down to the old house.

Mandie was used to getting up early. Back when her father was living, he was always the first one in the kitchen in the morning, making coffee and sometimes cooking breakfast. It had been Mandie's special time with her father.

When the old rooster crowed in the backyard the next morning, Mandie woke, stretched, and quickly dressed to go downstairs.

Pushing open the door to the kitchen she found Uncle John sitting at the table drinking coffee. He had a stack of business papers in front of him. As he looked up and saw her, Mandie quickly joined him at the table.

"Good morning. Where is everybody?" she asked.

"Well, it's a little early for Aunt Lou and the others to prepare breakfast," John Shaw replied. "I just slipped in here and made a pot of coffee. How about a cup?"

"I'll get it," Mandie said, rising to get a cup and saucer down from the cupboard. She took it over to the big iron cookstove, picked up the percolator, and filled the cup with hot coffee.

As she joined her uncle at the table, she asked, "Are you doing work? Am I hindering you?"

"Of course you are not interfering. I was just glancing through some papers that I need to sort out and file in my cabinet upstairs," he replied. "Now, tell me, did you see anything at the old house last night?"

Mandie's blue eyes sparkled as she replied, "Yes, sir, there is definitely someone in that house. Liza and I watched for a long time and never saw a light in it. Then we started back up the hill and when I turned to look back, there was a light. We rushed back down to look, but guess what happened? Snowball had followed me and came running all the way down to the old house." She stopped to sigh.

"And I know what happened next." John Shaw chuckled. "You chased him and the light went out because of the noise you made."

Mandie laughed. "You almost got it right. Only, it was Snowball who made the racket when he jumped up on the porch down there and ran into something. Then he went under the house and I had to poke him out with a stick. And of course the light went out when he made that noise. But there is definitely someone in that old house."

"Yes, I am pretty sure there is, too," John Shaw agreed. "And I don't want you going down there alone. We don't know what kind of person, or persons, are holed up in there."

"All right, I won't go back except when Liza can go with me," Mandie promised.

"I imagine with all the company coming, Aunt

Lou will keep Liza pretty busy," John Shaw told her. "Maybe when your friends get here you can all go investigating."

"Oh, Uncle John, they aren't coming till the weekend. I'd like to find out something before then. In fact, I don't have anything to do until they do get here."

"You are not to go down there alone, now, remember that," John Shaw told her. He looked at her sternly as he sipped his coffee.

"All right, Uncle John," Mandie said reluctantly. "Maybe I can talk Aunt Lou into letting Liza go with me."

Aunt Lou entered the kitchen at that moment and heard the remark. She smiled at Mandie and said, "Got lots of work fo' Liza to do today." She shook her head as she continued on across the room to get down pots and pans to begin the breakfast meal. "Y'all sho' are up early dis heah mawnin', my chile."

Mandie smiled at the big woman and said, "You know I always get up early, Aunt Lou. I believe you're just a little bit late this morning." She grinned as Aunt Lou turned to look at her.

"I sho' am," the woman replied. "Dat sun jes' didn't come up in dat sky to wake me up." She continued bustling around the kitchen.

"The sun didn't come up?" Mandie quickly questioned her and went to look out a window. "Looks like it might rain."

"I believe it sprinkled a little during the night," John Shaw said, looking up from his papers. "The ground was a little wet when I went outside earlier this morning."

"Where dat white cat, my chile? Don't see him

sittin' heah beggin' fo' food," Aunt Lou asked, glancing around the room.

"I don't know. He wasn't in my room when I got up. I figured he had already come down here," Mandie replied, also looking in the woodbox behind the stove.

"He'll show up soon as I git de food cooking," the old woman said.

Liza came into the kitchen at that moment. Snowball rushed past her and jumped into the woodbox. "Dat cat he come git on my bed last night," Liza told Mandie.

"All the way up to the third floor? I wonder how he found you," Mandie replied.

The girl laughed as she held out an empty bowl. "He smelt de food I took up to my room last night," she said. "I didn't eat all of it, but it sho' all gone dis mawnin'." She put the bowl in the sink.

"Why didn't you chase him out of your room?" Mandie asked.

"He wudn't hurtin' nuthin' so I figures he'd leave soon, but dis mawnin' he still dere, curled up on de foot of my bed," Liza replied.

"Liza, git de table set in de dinin' room, quick-like befo' Miz Taft and Miz 'Lizbeth come down," Aunt Lou told the girl.

Liza quickly went to the dish cabinet.

John Shaw stood up and picked up his papers. "I'm leaving, Aunt Lou," he said. "I don't want to interfere with your work. And I've got to look for something in my office anyway."

"I'll get out of the way, too," Mandie said as she rose from the table and took her coffee cup to the sink.

"What's all dis heah leavin' bidness? Ain't no-body in my way," Aunt Lou grumbled as she filled a pot with water to boil for the grits.

"I'll be back—for the food, that is," John Shaw said, grinning at the old woman as he left the room.

"I will, too, but, Aunt Lou, do you think Liza might have any time free that she could go down and watch the old house with me today? You see, Uncle John said I couldn't go by myself," Mandie said, turning to look at the woman.

Aunt Lou set the pot full of water on the stove and turned to put an arm around Mandie standing nearby. "I see whut we kin do, my chile. You axe me agin aftuh breakfast." She gave Mandie a squeeze.

Mandie reached to quickly embrace the woman and stepped back, saying, "Thank you, Aunt Lou. I knew I could depend on you."

As it turned out, Aunt Lou couldn't spare Liza because of the sudden arrival of more guests. But that pleased Mandie to no end because the new arrivals were none other than Dr. and Mrs. Woodard and Joe.

Jenny, the cook, had come to finish up breakfast, and everyone was sitting in the dining room when there was a loud knock on the front door. Liza went hurrying to answer it and came back shortly to usher the Woodards into the dining room.

Mandie looked up from her plate in surprise. As everyone was exchanging greetings, she had eyes for Joe only. And he came directly to the table where she sat.

"Hello, I'm glad you're here already," Joe told her.

Mandie pushed back her chair and rose. "Oh, Joe, what a nice surprise," she said, feeling a little shy. Joe Woodard seemed to have grown a foot since she last saw him at Christmas, and he looked so much more mature, and good-looking, too, Mandie silently noted.

Everyone was talking at once as Elizabeth Shaw saw to seating her new guests. Joe, of course, ended up next to Mandie, and Mandie suddenly lost her appetite for some strange reason. She sat there with her finger in the handle of her coffee cup and tried to think of something to say.

Joe, on the other hand, was full of conversation and began talking instead of eating, which was very unusual for him.

"My father needs to check on patients in this area, and we plan to stay the whole two weeks here," he told Mandie. "We'll be going home at the end of next week just in time for me to get my things and get on my way back to college."

"Celia and her mother and her aunt are coming this weekend," Mandie told him without looking straight into his brown eyes.

"That will be nice seeing Celia again," Joe said, turning to take a bite of food from his plate. "And I suppose you've already found a mystery to solve while you're home."

That broke the tension, and Mandie quickly looked at him and said, "Oh, Joe, there's this old house down at the creek just over Uncle John's property line that someone is staying in and nobody knows who it is."

Mandie explained about the light and the fact that no one had seen anyone down there. Also, that John Shaw had forbidden her to go down there alone and Liza was going to be too busy.

"So you came at the exact right time," Mandie told him, sipping her coffee.

"Oh, Mandie, can't we ever do anything but chase mysteries?" Joe said, reaching to hold her hand.

Mandie quickly pulled her hand away and picked

up her fork. "But there are always mysteries every-where I go," she said and turned away.

"And if there aren't any, you sure can find one," Joe teased, grinning as he leaned to look into her face.

"Well . . . anyhow," Mandie stuttered. "Are you interested in helping me find out what is going on at that old house or not?"

"It's like this," Joe replied. "If I want to see you, I suppose I'll have to follow you around on this mys-tery."

So Joe followed her down to look at that old house after breakfast was over. The sky was still cloudy and threatening to drop its rain down on them. A chilly wind was blowing, and Mandie was glad she had worn her cloak.

When they came within sight of the old house, Mandie put her hand out to stop Joe. "Let's not go any closer, because whoever is in there will definitely see us, but if we stay here behind the trunks of those trees, maybe they won't spot us and will come out-side," she explained. "The ground is too wet to sit down."

Stepping off the pathway, Mandie went to lean against a huge tree trunk, and Joe followed.

Joe, still looking down at the house, asked, "Do you mean someone is living in that old barn? Looks like it's ready to fall in."

"I know, but there has been a light in there sev-eral times, according to Uncle John, and Liza and I saw it last night," Mandie replied.

"But this is daytime," Joe said. "Do you think they'd have a light on in the daytime?"

"I imagine so because all the shutters are closed that I can see, and that would make it dark inside," Mandie said. She continued watching the house and moved slightly away from Joe around the tree trunk.

Joe moved a little closer and said, "It's really hard to see the whole house from this spot. Maybe we should move on down the hill a little. What do you think?"

Mandie moved slightly backward as she replied, "I'm afraid whoever it is in there might see us and then they'd never come out."

"But we could go through the bushes over there for a long distance yet without coming out into the open," Joe said, pointing to the thick growth down the hill on each side of the pathway.

"Well, I suppose we could," Mandie reluctantly agreed. She realized there were no large trees along the hill and that meant she would have to stay closer to Joe behind the bushes to keep from being seen.

"Here, I'll go first and hold back the branches for you to get through," Joe said, stepping down the hill.

"Just don't go too fast. This is a steep hill," Mandie cautioned him as she followed.

Joe offered her his hand, but Mandie ignored it and held on to the bushes instead as she stepped down. Now and then she glanced in the direction of the house, which she could see as she moved between bushes. There was still no sign of anyone down there.

When they came to the last of the bushes, Mandie stopped and whispered, for fear of being heard by anyone who might be in the house now that they were so close, "We'd better stop right here or someone will see us for sure if we step out of the bushes."

"Right," Joe agreed and came to stand by her side. Then he added, "Don't you think we ought to just go down there and knock on the door?"

"Oh no, that wouldn't ever do," Mandie quickly

replied. "Whoever is inside that house doesn't want anyone to see them, that's for sure."

"But we might just stand here all day with nothing happening," Joe argued.

Mandie looked up at him and grinned. "Then we'll just keep on coming back until whoever that is comes outside," she said.

Joe ran his hand through his unruly brown hair and said, "What a way to spend the holidays."

"But just think what satisfaction it would be to solve this mystery," Mandie replied, her blue eyes twinkling as she gazed into his brown ones.

"We do get time off to go back and eat now and then, don't we?" Joe teased.

A strong puff of wind came down the hill right then, and there was a loud banging noise at the old house. Mandie and Joe both quickly straightened up to look down the hill. There was no one in sight.

"Oh, shucks! Must have been the wind banging a shutter or something," Mandie said in disappointment.

"Maybe the wind will just bang one of them off so we can see inside," Joe said, teasing her again.

Another stronger gust of wind blew through the bushes. Mandie quickly looked down the hill again. "Shucks, that one didn't even rattle the shutter," she said.

All of a sudden it began raining. Mandie quickly pulled the hood of her cloak over her head and turned to go back up the hill. "Guess we'd better get back to the house," she said.

"Yes," Joe agreed, following her.

Halfway up the slope Mandie suddenly slipped and Joe caught her. "I believe you'd better let me hold your hand," he said, grasping her hand tightly.

"Oh, all right, then," Mandie agreed reluctantly.

They got to the front porch of John Shaw's house and stomped their feet to clean off the water and mud. Mandie shook her cloak and said, "I think I'd like to go dry out by the fire."

"Good idea," Joe agreed as he opened the front door for her.

Mandie was surprised to find that no one was in the parlor. Where was everyone, she wondered as she hurriedly left her cloak on the hall tree and went to stand by the blazing fire in the fireplace.

Joe followed her and sat on a stool nearby.

At that moment Liza came into the room. "Jes' checkin' to see how dat fire be comin'," she told them, reaching to put another log on the fire.

"I'll help you," Joe offered, taking the log and pitching it on the fire.

"Where is everybody, Liza?" Mandie asked.

"Ev'rybody dun gone ev'ry which way, dey has," Liza replied. "Mistuh John went off in de buggy wid de doctuh man. Den Miz 'Lizbeth gits Abraham to hitch up de rig and he drives huh and Miz Taft and Miz Woodard off someplace or other. Didn't heah dem say where."

Mandie looked at the girl and smiled. "Are you all caught up with your work, then?" she asked.

"Jes' fo' a few minutes," Liza replied. "But dat don't make no never mind 'cause it be rainin' out dere and we cain't go down to spy on dat house in de rain, dat's fo' sho'."

"That's where we've been," Joe told her. "And we got all wet."

"Oh well, maybe everyone will come back soon because it is raining," Mandie said.

"Dey tell Aunt Lou they be back fo' dinner. Twelve noon sharp, Miz 'Lizbeth say," Liza replied. "Now I got to go set dat table."

"Liza, if you get caught up and the rain stops, you can go back with us to watch that house later," Mandie told her.

"I sho' am plannin' on it," the girl said as she left the room.

Mandie sat down on the other stool by the fireplace and said, "I do wonder where everyone went. It's strange they all left at about the same time."

"Oh, Mandie, I can explain part of that, I believe," Joe said, grinning. "Your uncle probably went with my father to make some calls on his patients. Remember I told you he had to call on some of them while he's here?"

Mandie nodded and said, "Yes, but where in the world would our mothers and my grandmother all go together? I didn't hear any of them mention going off anyplace, did you?"

Joe sat back and grinned again. "Always looking for a mystery," he teased. "And you'll probably find out they merely went to a store, or something like that."

"Well, anyhow, no one told me they were going off," Mandie said with a frown.

"But they knew we were down there watching the old house, I'm sure," Joe replied. Clearing his throat, he asked, "Now, tell me, what have you and Celia been up to at school since I saw y'all?"

Mandie smiled and said, "Nothing much at all, believe it or not. Things got kinda dull after we got in trouble about that dark alley."

Joe frowned and said seriously, "That could have been an awfully bad experience for you girls." Then smiling, he added, "That taught you a lesson, I hope."

"Well, that particular lesson, I suppose, for that particular mystery," Mandie admitted. Then she smiled and said, "But that didn't change my mind about solving mysteries whenever I run into one. I'll just have to be more careful from now on."

"I agree with that," Joe said. "And, Mandie, you know that could be an outlaw, or someone like that, hiding out in that old house."

"I know. Uncle John has already reminded me of that," Mandie replied, shifting her long skirts in front of the fire to get the dampness off. "But I'm sure you and I will be able to find out before you leave here. Also, Celia will join us this weekend."

"Well, I hope we can solve this one and put an end to it so we can enjoy doing something else while we're all here," Joe said.

"We will," Mandie promised.

She was already trying to think of ways to find out who was in that old house. She would come up with some solution.

Chapter 4 / Missing

Mandie moved around in front of the fireplace, still trying to dry her long skirts, as she and Joe discussed the old house and possible occupants. Joe stretched his long legs out to get rid of the dampness from the rain as he sat on the stool.

"You will go back down there with me, won't you, when it stops raining?" Mandie asked with a smile.

"Well, all right, but mind you, there's no telling how long this rain will last," Joe replied, grinning at her.

Mandie heard the front door open and close and she stepped to the doorway to look out into the hall. Glancing back at Joe, she whispered, "My mother, your mother, and Grandmother have returned."

"I believe I will go on up to my room and change clothes," Mrs. Taft was saying as she walked down the hallway.

"Did y'all get wet?" Mandie asked as her mother and Mrs. Woodard started to follow Mrs. Taft.

"A little," Mrs. Woodard responded, walking toward the staircase.

"I'm glad to see you are not out in the rain, Amanda," Elizabeth Shaw told her daughter. "I'll be right back to the parlor. Amanda, will you please ask

Liza to bring coffee for us?"

"Yes, ma'am," Mandie replied. Turning back to Joe, she said, "I'll be right back." And she hurried toward the kitchen.

Mandie found only Aunt Lou there. She was chopping up onions.

"Oh, I can't get too close to you, Aunt Lou, or those onions will get in my eyes, but my mother and Grandmother and Mrs. Woodard just came home, and Mother wanted me to ask Liza to bring coffee to the parlor. They've all gone upstairs to change clothes and will be back down shortly."

"We sho' will get coffee and some sweet cakes in dere shortly," the old woman replied, pausing to squint her eyes against the onions. "You don't be knowin' where dat Liza has got to, does you, my chile?"

"Last I saw her, she said she had to set the table for the noon meal," Mandie said.

"I done checked de dinin' room. Table set but Liza not dere." Aunt Lou said, chopping more onions.

"Maybe she's upstairs," Mandie suggested. "I'll go look for her."

At that moment Jenny, the cook, came in the back door.

"I'll send de coffee by Jenny, my chile. You go see if you kin find Liza and tell huh to git on in heah right now," Aunt Lou said and, turning to the cook, added, "Miz 'Lizbeth and de ladies, dey be back and be wantin' coffee in de parlor."

"Yessum, dat I'll take care of," Jenny replied, going toward the stove.

"I'll let you know if I find Liza," Mandie promised.

She hurried back down the hallway to the parlor. "Guess what? Liza is missing," she said with a knowing grin. "Want to guess where she is?"

Joe stood up, stretched, and smiled as he replied, "Down at the old house? She's as bad about mysteries as you are, Mandie."

"I told Aunt Lou I would look for her," Mandie said. "I don't want to . . ." she paused as she heard the front door open and close. Rushing to the doorway, she saw Liza come in.

"Missy 'Manda, please don't be tellin' I been out in dat rain, or Aunt Lou, she'll skin me alive," Liza quickly told her as she came down the hallway. She shook the cloak she was wearing and took it off.

Mandie noticed that underneath the cloak Liza was not wet. Therefore, no one would know where the girl had been. "I won't go back and tell Aunt Lou anything," she told the girl. "But you had better hurry back to the kitchen because she is looking for you."

"I make haste," Liza said, stepping into a room down the hall and leaving the cloak inside. She closed the door and looked back at Mandie and said, "Still ain't seed nuthin' down at dat house, but we'se gwine keep lookin', ain't we?" She grinned and started toward the kitchen door.

"Yes," Mandie called to her.

Turning back inside the parlor, Mandie went to sit by the fireplace. "You heard, didn't you?" she asked Joe.

"I heard, and I hope no one else heard or Liza may be in deep trouble with Aunt Lou," Joe replied with a big grin.

Mandie heard the front door open again and went to look out into the hallway. This time it was her uncle John and Dr. Woodard, shaking rain off their clothes and hanging up their hats and coats.

John Shaw glanced at Mandie and said, "It's a

little wet out there." He smiled.

"I'd say that's an understatement," Dr. Woodard said. "And it looks like it might keep on."

"Y'all come on in here by the fire. Aunt Lou is sending coffee shortly because Mother and Grandmother and Mrs. Woodard are also back."

The fireplace in the parlor was huge and wide enough for several chairs to be placed in front of it. The two men came in, pulled up chairs, and sat down before it.

Elizabeth, Mrs. Taft, and Mrs. Woodard returned downstairs and came in to join everyone in the parlor.

Then, just as Mandie was about to inform them coffee was on the way, Liza appeared in the doorway with the tea cart. The aroma of hot coffee and freshly baked sweet cakes filled the room.

Elizabeth filled cups and passed them around with Liza's help.

"So you ladies went out, too," John Shaw remarked, sipping the hot coffee in his cup.

"Yes, we thought we'd go by the Harrisons' and invite them to our dinner party, and then on to the Sullivans' house, and by that time it was pouring, so we came back," Elizabeth explained.

"But we at least gave them the invitation, and they will be coming," Mrs. Taft added.

"Well, I do hope it clears up by Friday night," Mrs. Woodard said.

John Shaw smiled and said, "I don't believe a little rain will prevent those people from coming."

"And don't forget," Mandie said. "Celia and her mother and her aunt Rebecca will be arriving Friday. I sure hope it doesn't rain all during our holidays."

"I have a feeling a little rain won't stop you and your friends from enjoying the holidays." John Shaw smiled at her. "Even if you have to camp out in it to watch that old house."

"But it would make it awfully uncomfortable to stay out there and get soaking wet," Mandie replied with a grin.

"I just remembered something," John Shaw said. "There is an old rose arbor on the other side of the pathway down the hill, and I'm sure you could see that old house from there. Now, if y'all could figure out how to rig up a covering over the arbor, you could stay out of the rain."

Mandie excitedly replied, "Oh, that's a wonderful idea, Uncle John!" Turning to Joe she said, "Will you help me cover it?"

"With what?" Joe asked.

"I believe there are several large pieces of wood from some old crates in the barn, which you could use to make a roof over it," John Shaw told him.

"Oh no! Work on my holidays!" Joe pretended to be upset.

"Work never hurt any man," Dr. Woodard spoke up.

"I'll help you," John Shaw volunteered.

"Are you planning on doing this in the rain?" Joe asked.

John Shaw smiled and replied, "Not today. I thought we'd wait and see what the weather's like tomorrow, and if it lets up long enough we could get it done then."

"Thank you, sir," Joe answered with a big smile as he glanced at Mandie.

Mandie knew what Joe was thinking, and that was that she never wanted to waste any time when it came to tracking down a mystery. But this time she was not anxious to venture out in the rain again, so she only smiled back at Joe. Then she had another idea.

Turning to Joe, she said, "You know the exit from the secret tunnel comes out down at the creek. I wonder if that exit is anywhere near the old house, or whether we could see that house from there."

Joe blew out his breath and replied, "Mandie, you just get too many ideas about these things. I don't know if the house could be seen from there or not, but remember we would have to go all the way down through the tunnel to get to the exit, unless we walked in the rain outside, and that would not be a good idea."

"Let's go find out," Mandie said, starting to rise from the stool where she had been sitting.

"Now? Let's wait until after we eat," Joe protested.

Mandie glanced at the clock. A little over an hour until noontime, when Aunt Lou would have dinner ready. That wouldn't give them enough time. "All right," she agreed. "As soon as we eat let's go find out." She pushed back her long blond hair tied with a ribbon.

"If you insist," Joe reluctantly agreed.

The noon meal turned out to be a long, drawn-out affair. All the adults carried on a conversation about any and everything and of no interest to Mandie and Joe. Mandie kept wishing they would hurry up and finish eating so they could check out the secret tunnel that ran under the house. Her great-grandfather had built the tunnel to hide his Cherokee friends from the white people who had taken everything the Indians had and herded them out of the state. Her own grandmother had been a full-blooded Cherokee, which made Mandie one-fourth and a staunch defender of Cherokee rights.

"Wake up!" Joe teased her.

Mandie shook her head to clear her thoughts and smiled at him. "I wasn't exactly sleeping."

"I know, you were dreaming about that tunnel, whether you could see that old house from the exit or not," Joe said, grinning at her.

Mandie felt as though he had read her thoughts. She cleared her throat and said, "Well, partly."

"And what is the other part, then?" Joe asked.

"I don't think I ought to tell you," she teased.

"Well, now I must know," he insisted. Leaning toward her, he added, "Please?"

Mandie moved slightly away from him as she replied, "No, you must not know." She felt that shy feeling coming back again. Joe, who had been her lifelong friend, seemed to have turned into a different person since he had been away at the university in New Orleans this school year. She was not exactly comfortable around him like in the old days. And then it dawned on her. Joe had turned into a different person from the boy she had always walked to school with, the boy who had always shared her joys and sorrows. Somehow he now seemed to be so much older and more mature. She was losing her old friendship feeling with Joe and she didn't exactly like it or know what to do about it. That college was changing him. Oh, why did he have to go away to finish school?

"You haven't answered me yet," Joe said, leaning closer.

Suddenly she blurted out in spite of herself, "I don't think I like colleges." And she moved away from him.

"Well, now, what have you got against colleges?" he asked, plainly puzzled. "You will have to go to college yourself after you graduate from the

Heathwood's School next year, you know."

"I know, and I don't like the idea," Mandie replied, nervously moving the silverware around her plate.

"Pray tell me, what is it about college that you don't like?" Joe asked, trying to look her straight in the face as she moved about in her chair.

"It . . . it . . . ah . . . makes people different, changes them somehow," she stuttered in reply.

"Sure it does," he agreed. "With more education it expands your knowledge and sometimes changes the way you think, your beliefs, and your hopes for the future."

"But I don't want my friends to change. I like them the way they are," Mandie told him.

"Aha!" Joe exclaimed. "You think I've changed. Not really. I still belong to Charley Gap in the Nantahala Mountains, just like you always will, no matter what we ever learn or do. Those are our roots and we can't just pull up roots and decide to turn into something different. I think what you are seeing or thinking is that we are both growing up and changing to a certain degree with age, but you and I will always be just plain Mandie and Joe. Nothing could ever change that." He leaned closer still and smiled.

"Maybe it has already changed and we just haven't noticed it," Mandie suggested, trying not to look Joe straight in the eyes.

"Then maybe the change is for the better," Joe teased.

"I don't think so," Mandie said, drawing out the words slowly and frowning as she looked up into his face.

"Oh, but just think of how different it is when you are grown up and educated," Joe reminded her. Then he leaned over to whisper in her ear, "I still want to marry you when we grow up, Mandie, and growing up is going pretty fast."

When Mandie dropped her gaze to her plate and did not answer, Joe added, "I meant that when I first asked you the day your mother married your uncle John."

"That was a long time ago," Mandie reminded him. "And we were both so much younger then."

Joe cleared his throat and asked, "Have you definitely decided then that you do not want to marry me when the proper time comes?"

"No, Joe, I haven't decided yes or no about anything," Mandie said.

"Then I'll keep hoping," he said, reaching to squeeze her hand, and this time she did not pull away.

Elizabeth Shaw stood up and asked, "Shall we take our coffee in the parlor where we can sit by the fire?" She looked around the table.

Everyone agreed. Liza, who was tending the sideboard, turned to say, "Den we git de coffee and cake in dere right away, Miz 'Lizbeth."

"Thank you," Elizabeth replied, leading the way out of the dining room.

"Did I hear Liza say cake?" Joe asked as he and Mandie rose to follow the others.

Mandie laughed and said, "Cake, of course. And with Joe Woodard here it's sure to be chocolate. Let's go."

Glancing at Liza as he passed her on the way out, he whispered, "Liza, please hurry with that chocolate cake." He grinned at her.

"Sho' 'nuff, I will," Liza replied, grinning back.

As everyone sat in the parlor enjoying the cake and coffee, Mandie looked around and said, "I haven't seen Snowball in a while. I wonder where he is."

Joe glanced around the floor and replied, "I haven't, either."

"Wherever there's food, he finds the way to get near it," Mandie said, frowning. "I think I'll just go look in the kitchen and see if he's in there. I'll be right back." She set her cup of coffee on the end table and left the room.

When she pushed open the kitchen door, she found all the servants inside, getting ready for their own noon meal.

Aunt Lou looked at her and asked, "What be de matter, my chile?"

"I'm just checking to see where Snowball is. Have y'all seen him lately?" she asked, walking across the room to look in the woodbox.

"No" was the unanimous answer.

"Not since breakfast," Aunt Lou added. "I remember giving him his food and den he jes' hightailed it out of heah soon as someone opened de do'."

"And Joe and I went outside. Mother and the others went visiting. And Dr. Woodard and Uncle John were also gone. We were all gone at one time, and I imagine he tried to follow some of us," Mandie said, standing there in the kitchen, trying to remember when she had last seen him.

"I git Liza to he'p you look fo' him, my chile," Aunt Lou said. "He 'round heah somewhere. Maybe got shut up in a room or something."

"Thanks, Aunt Lou, but y'all go ahead and have your dinner first," Mandie said. "When Liza gets finished I'll be in the parlor."

When Mandie entered the parlor, her mother looked up to see who was coming in.

"Snowball is missing, Mother," Mandie spoke across the room, and everyone else stopped talking to listen. "Liza is going to help me look for him as soon as she finishes her dinner. But have y'all seen him today anywhere?"

No one had, and Mandie sat back down next to Joe.

"He's around somewhere," Joe said. "We'll find him."

"I hope nothing has happened to him," Mandie said. "I always keep thinking about that time when he came home half dead and we never did know where he had been. He almost died, remember?" Her blue eyes glistened with tears.

Joe reached to hold her hand. "I remember," he said. "But this time I believe we'll find him close by somewhere, maybe shut up accidentally in a room."

"That's what Aunt Lou said, but we'll see," Mandie replied.

Snowball was precious to Mandie. He was no ordinary cat. She had brought him with her as a tiny kitten when her stepmother sent her away from home after her father had died several years ago.

Uncle John came over to sit by Mandie and told her, "Don't worry too much. You know that cat likes to hide and play tricks. I'll help y'all search the house."

Mandie squeezed his hand and said, "Oh, thank you, Uncle John. I was hoping someone would volunteer to search the basement because Liza is afraid of it and I don't really like the place myself." She smiled at him.

"Yes, it is rather dark and spooky down there, isn't it? But I know every crack and corner of it in the dark," John Shaw replied, returning her smile. "So you and Liza look through the house. It's so big that will take a while. And Joe will help me."

Mandie remembered something. "Liza said he went all the way up to the third floor last night and got on her bed, so maybe he has gone back up there," she said.

"Then you should look there first," Joe suggested. "This house is so big and there are so many places he could hide, this will take a while, as Mr. Shaw said."

"Snowball will come if you call him as you go through the house. That is, if he can hear you and is not shut up somewhere," Mandie said.

She fidgeted in her chair and was not able to carry on a conversation about anything because of worry about her cat. And it seemed that Liza was taking an awfully long time to eat her dinner. The poor cat could be in trouble somewhere and in need of help. Then she remembered her favorite Bible verse in time of trouble.

Silently reaching for Joe's hand as John Shaw went back across the room, she whispered, "Our verse," and he understood.

Together they quoted, " 'What time I am afraid I will put my trust in Thee.' "

Then as they looked at each other and smiled, Mandie said, "Everything is going to be all right."

Chapter 5 / Searching

The afternoon was spent searching the house for Snowball without any results. Everyone finished and met in the back hallway.

"He is not in the house," Mandie decided.

"He's probably out chasing a bird somewhere," John Shaw suggested.

"And gittin' sloppy wet," Liza added. "And dat cat he don't like to git wet so I cain't figger why he outside in de rain."

Mandie quickly glanced at Liza. The girl was right. Snowball did not like rain and had to be coaxed to go outside in wet weather. He would rather curl up in the woodbox behind the big iron cookstove in the kitchen.

"Neither can I," Mandie agreed.

"Maybe he followed us out this morning when we went down the hill to look at that old house," Joe suggested.

"If he did, we should have had a glimpse of him somewhere or other while we were outside," Mandie replied. She quickly made a decision and said, "I'll just have to go out in that rain and look for him."

"I'll go with you," Joe offered.

"Me too," Liza added. "Dat is if Aunt Lou say I kin."

Mandie smiled at the girl and said, "I'll ask her if you want me to."

"Sho' 'nuff, you do dat," Liza agreed.

"You don't need me for that, so I should get back to our guests," John Shaw told Mandie. "Just don't stay out too long and be sure you change clothes immediately when you come back inside. We don't want you coming down with a cold, especially with your company coming Friday."

"Yes, sir, Uncle John," Mandie replied, too worried about her cat to smile at Uncle John's remarks.

After getting Aunt Lou's permission for Liza to go outside with her and Joe, the three put on their coats and hats, and Mandie picked up an umbrella from the hall tree to carry outside.

As soon as they stepped off the front porch, Mandie knew the umbrella would be useless because of the strong wind. She let it down and used it as a walking cane through rough spots in the yard.

They called and called Snowball's name, but there was no sign of the white cat. After they had searched the grounds around the house, they drifted down the hill in the direction of the old house.

"This is slippery," Mandie complained as she felt her foot slide on a muddy spot. She looked at Liza and said, "You had better be careful, Liza. If you fall down in all this mud and mess up your clothes you know what Aunt Lou will do."

Liza grinned at her as she moved alongside Joe and said, "Don't worry none 'bout dat, Missy 'Manda. I'se dun got too old to spank."

"Yes, but there are other ways to be punished. Remember the time Aunt Lou made you scrub all the floors because you had tracked in a little dirt?" Mandie reminded her.

"I 'member dat but I don't be trackin' in no mo'

mud 'cause I knows bettuh now," Liza replied, still grinning.

When the old house came into view, Mandie stopped to stare at it. The daylight was fast fading away because of the rainy weather, but she could still make out the shuttered window and the door. No light was showing from inside.

Joe moved over next to her and said, "Mandie, I don't think we ought to stand out here in all this rain just to look at that old house."

Mandie turned to go back up the hill. "I know. I thought maybe since we were this close to it we might spot a light," she said.

"Even if we see a light in there we can't do anything about it," Joe reminded her. "We can't just go up and knock on the door."

Mandie silently nodded her head as the three climbed back up the hill. When they stepped up on the front porch of the house, Mandie remembered something she had wanted to do.

"We never did go through the tunnel to see if we could see that old house from the exit like we planned for this afternoon, remember?" she said to Joe.

"I know," Joe replied. "But since Snowball is more important, I didn't bother to remind you about it. We can do that tomorrow if you want to."

"All right," Mandie agreed.

"Y'all gwine down in dat dahk tunnel place?" Liza asked.

"Yes, we are," Joe replied with a big grin. "You want to go with us? We're only going to walk through it to where it ends down by the creek."

"Not me." Liza shrugged her shoulders and reached to open the front door. "Ain't nuthin' in dat place I wants to see."

"Come on, let's all go get into some dry clothes," Mandie suggested as she stepped inside the hallway.

Liza started toward the kitchen near which the back stairway went up to the servants' quarters. "If y'all git a notion to go look at dat house again tonight, would y'all let me go wid you?" she asked.

"Sure, Liza, we'll let you know," Joe replied.

"But I'm pretty sure we won't be going back outside tonight," Mandie added.

After Mandie washed up and changed clothes in her room, she came down to the parlor and found that Joe was there ahead of her. Evidently he had told everyone about their failure to find Snowball, because as she entered the room she was greeted with remarks about it.

"That's a nice healthy cat you've got, so I wouldn't worry about him. He'll come back home when he gets ready," Dr. Woodard told her.

"Yes, cats like to prowl," Mrs. Woodard added.

"You should have left him at my house, Amanda, as I suggested," Mrs. Taft said.

"Now, you know Amanda and her cat can't be parted," John Shaw reminded the lady. Turning to Mandie, he added, "He'll get lonesome and come on back."

"Amanda, I'm sorry you can't find him. He's probably run off into the woods chasing something or other," Elizabeth told her.

"Thanks, everybody," Mandie quickly said as soon as she was able to get a chance to speak. Turning to her mother, she asked, "What are we planning to do while Celia and her mother and her aunt are here? Anything special?"

Elizabeth looked at her in surprise and replied, "Just the dinner party, dear. I thought you and Celia and Joe would find things to do on your own. Now, I could probably figure out something else if you'd like."

"Why, yes, we could, Amanda," Mrs. Taft spoke up quickly. "We could have another dinner party on Saturday night and invite other friends."

Mandie quickly smiled and said, "Oh no, no, Grandmother. I was only asking about Mother's plans so I'd know what I could plan for Celia and me. If the rain goes away there are lots of things to do. We could walk over to see the Burnses." Turning to her uncle, she asked, "Are they still living in that house over there and working for you?"

"Yes, they are, and they've turned out to be good workers," John Shaw replied. "I'm glad I gave them a chance to get straightened out from their old crooked ways."

"They're good people now that they've settled down," Elizabeth added. "Mrs. Burns helps me with a lot of work around the house here when we have extra company."

"I believe Polly Cornwallis and her mother went somewhere for the holidays so they probably won't be home," Mandie continued. The Cornwallises were the Shaws' next-door neighbors, and Polly went to the same boarding school that Mandie attended.

"And y'all can always drive out to the ruby mine," John Shaw added.

"Yes, we could," Mandie agreed. "We will find plenty of things to do. Time always flies by on holidays."

Mrs. Woodard spoke up. "I do believe I forgot to tell y'all, and I'm sorry, but Mr. Jacob Smith came by before we left home and said to tell y'all he might just drop by while everyone is here."

Mandie's eyes lit up as she excitedly said, "Oh, I hope he does. I haven't seen him in quite a while and I'd like to know how things are at my father's house."

Her father's house was over at Charley Gap in Swain County between the Nantahala Mountains. After Mandie got control of the house when he died, she had given Mr. Jacob Smith permission to live there and take care of the place for her since she could not live there anytime soon.

"Yes, it would be nice to have him come visit," John Shaw added.

At that moment Liza came to the doorway and announced, "De supper be on de table, Miz 'Lizbeth," and then quickly walked on.

Elizabeth rose and said, "Shall we go eat now?"

"Is it time for supper? Seems like no time since we had dinner," Mrs. Woodard remarked as she and Mrs. Taft followed.

"Doesn't seem like no time to me," Joe whispered to Mandie as they got up.

Dr. Woodard bent close as he passed them and said, "I heard that, Joe. You just remember your manners and don't overeat." The old man winked at Mandie.

During the meal the adults carried on their own conversation. Joe did all the talking to Mandie, who was unusually quiet because of her worry about Snowball. She didn't listen to half of what Joe was saying as he related stories about his life at the college in New Orleans and the town itself.

"Maybe you can come down sometime and I will take you around and show you the town. And you can meet all my friends at the college," Joe told her.

"Yes, I'd like to," Mandie replied.

"The weather is hotter in the summertime than it

is here," Joe continued. "Of course, we are in the mountains here and that makes it cooler. New Orleans is on the water, you know."

"Yes," Mandie answered, pushing the food around on her plate. She looked up, caught a concerned look on her mother's face, and quickly crammed a forkful of mashed potatoes into her mouth and washed it down with a sip of coffee.

"I suppose I'll be coming home for the summer," Joe continued. "Remember last year I had to double up on my studies to catch up for admission requirements and had to stay all summer?"

Mandie was interested in that. "I'm so glad you're coming home for the summer," she told him. "My grandmother has been asking me what I'm planning for the summer, and I haven't known what to tell her. You know how she likes to make plans for other people and always wants to get me involved."

"What are you planning to do for the summer, then?" Joe asked.

"I'd like to visit my Cherokee kinpeople," Mandie said.

"And come and stay at our house?" Joe asked.

"Probably," Mandie agreed. "Since you live practically on the way to Deep Creek."

"Maybe I could go with you to see all those people," Joe suggested.

"Of course, if you want to," Mandie replied, stopping to sip her coffee. "I have asked Celia, too, but you know her mother is always planning things for them and I'm not sure yet what their plans are."

"Will you write and let me know?" Joe asked.

"I will as soon as I find out," Mandie promised. "And you write and let me know exactly when you will be out of school for the summer."

"All right," Joe agreed.

The meal was finally over. When her mother rose from the table, Mandie immediately caught up with her before she left the dining room and said, "I'm going out on the porch to call Snowball."

"Be sure you stay on the porch and don't go out in that rain again. I don't want you getting sick," Elizabeth told her.

"Yes, ma'am," Mandie replied.

"I'll go with you," Joe said, having stood by listening.

The adults went on into the parlor. Mandie and Joe grabbed their coats off the hall tree and went out onto the front porch. The spring night air was cool and it was still raining.

Mandie walked up and down the long front porch calling, "Snowball! Kitty, kitty, where are you? Snowball, come here."

After a while, a discouraged Mandie and Joe went back inside and soon everyone went to bed.

Mandie thought about her cat as she drifted off to sleep. She dreamed she could hear him meowing. He seemed to be in trouble. Suddenly she woke up and sat straight up in bed. That wasn't a dream. She could distinctly hear Snowball howling his head off. But where was he?

She jumped out of bed, snatched her robe, and put it on as she ran down the stairs. She opened the front door and there he was, sitting there loudly meowing. He looked up, saw her, and quickly ran into the house.

"Snowball!" Mandie cried. She stooped down to pick him up. He was soaking wet.

As she ran up the stairs with him in her arms she realized he smelled awful. Some odor like fish reached her nostrils.

Once inside her room she quickly set him down,

closed the door, and lit a lamp. He was filthy dirty and smelled like something dead.

She picked him up, took him to the bathroom, and deposited him in the bathtub. Snowball was meowing the whole time, and she was sure he was going to wake everyone in the house. But he had to be cleaned so she turned on the water and bathed him, which made him howl louder than ever.

Finally picking him up in a towel, she sat down on the floor and tried to get him dry. Giving up trying to keep him still, she took a clean towel, rolled him up in it, carried him back to her room, and set him on a chair.

"Now, you stay right there. Don't you get in my bed. You're all wet, you understand?" she scolded him.

Snowball looked at her, managed to get his front feet out of the towel, and began washing his face.

Mandie put out the lamp, got back in bed, and waited to see what Snowball was going to do. Much to her surprise, he finally became quiet and as far as she could see in the darkness, he stayed in the chair, curled up, and went to sleep.

Happy that her cat had finally come home, Mandie drifted off to sleep. Now she could go back tomorrow to investigating the mystery of the light in the old house across the property line. And she and Joe could go down through the tunnel to find out whether they could see the place from the exit. But maybe it wouldn't be raining tomorrow.

Sometime during the night, Snowball slipped up onto her bed and curled up on the other pillow.

Mandie dreamed she could hear the wind roaring and woke in the middle of the night to find Snowball purring in her ear. As she moved to push him away, she remembered his fur was wet, but when she touched him it was dry. And he was back home. She turned over and went back to sleep.

Chapter 6 / Planning

Mandie woke early the next morning and opened her eyes to bright sunlight streaming in through the window. She sat up quickly. Had she overslept? She ran to the window to look out. No, the sun just seemed brighter because the previous day had been so dark. The rooster crowed in the backyard. She stretched and turned to look for Snowball. He was not in the room. Now where had he gone?

"Oh, that cat!" she moaned to herself as she hastily got dressed. "I'm going to tie him up if he doesn't stop running off."

She went straight to the kitchen. That's where he would go, but how did he get out of her room? John Shaw was sitting at the table drinking coffee and reading a newspaper. No one else was there.

"Good morning, my little blue eyes," her uncle greeted her. "Coffee's ready."

Mandie quickly got a cup and saucer, poured coffee from the percolator on the cookstove, and came to sit at the table with him.

"Snowball came home in the middle of the night and now he has disappeared out of my room with the door shut," Mandie said with a loud groan.

John Shaw grinned at her, pointed toward the floor behind the stove, and said, "I know. There he is, already eating his breakfast. Liza brought him in just a few minutes ago."

"Oh! How did Liza get him out of my room without waking me?" Mandie asked.

"She said she was going down the hallway up there and heard Snowball meowing inside the door of your room, and when she peeked inside he ran out," John Shaw explained. "She didn't wake you because she was sure you were 'done wore out.' "

Mandie quickly related the happenings of the night before when Snowball showed up at the front door. "I mean he was absolutely filthy and he smelled like fish," she said.

"He probably got hungry and tried to catch a fish out of the creek," John Shaw suggested.

"But I can't figure out where he has been, and since he can't talk I suppose I'll never know," Mandie concluded with a big sigh. She sipped the hot coffee and thought about it.

Joe came into the kitchen and joined them for coffee at the table. When Mandie related the story to him, he asked, "But how in the world could you have heard Snowball howling outside the front door? The front door is quite a distance from your room, I believe."

"That's because I was listening for him all the time, trying to hear his meow, and I thought I was dreaming, but I got up and went downstairs and there he was," Mandie explained.

Joe shrugged his shoulders and said, "Oh well, I'm certainly glad he decided to come home."

"And now I'm afraid he will run away again," Mandie said thoughtfully.

"Don't let him out of the house," John Shaw told her. "Inform everyone that he is not to go outside.

That way they'll be watching for him when they open outside doors."

"I suppose I could put on his leash and take him out for air with me," Mandie said. "You know the sun is shining." She smiled as she glanced toward the window.

"Yes, I'm glad it has cleared up," John Shaw said. Turning to Joe, he said, "Now would be a good time to put the cover on that rose arbor before it rains again."

"Yes, sir, I agree," Joe said. "Just let me know when."

"How about right after breakfast?" John Shaw suggested, drinking the last of his coffee.

"That will be fine," Joe agreed.

Liza came in the back door and smiled at Mandie. "I sees dat white cat dun come home agin," she said.

"Finally," Mandie replied and told her the events of the night before.

"Thank de Lawd," Liza said, rolling her dark eyes.

"Yes, and as soon as breakfast is over we're going to cover the arbor in case it rains again," Mandie replied.

"Dat's good to stay out of de rain, 'cause it sho' was rainin' last night when I seed a light down dere," Liza told her as she went to the stove and began taking down pots and pans in preparation for breakfast.

"Last night? You saw a light down there last night?" Mandie quickly asked. "You were out last night?"

Liza put her hand over her mouth and said, "I dun put my foot in trouble if Aunt Lou find out. Lawsy mercy, Missy 'Manda, I better keep my big mouth shut."

Joe grinned and said, "I do believe I'm getting hard of hearing this morning. What were you telling us about last night?"

Liza grinned back at him and said, "I ain't sayin' 'nuther word. I'se got to git breakfast started now." She turned back to the stove.

"I heard you, Liza, but I'm not telling," Mandie said. Turning to Uncle John, she said, "So there was a light down there last night. I do wish I could find out who's in that old house."

"We'll eventually find out," John Shaw replied, standing up from the table. "Right now I have a couple of things to do in my office before we eat breakfast. So I'll be back down to eat, Joe, and then we'll see about that arbor cover." After putting his cup in the sink, he went to the door to the hallway.

"Yes, sir, whenever you are ready," Joe agreed. As John Shaw left the room, Joe also stood up and said to Mandie, "I think we ought to go to the parlor before Aunt Lou comes in here. She might want to ask questions that we don't want to answer." He nodded toward Liza and left his cup next to John Shaw's.

Mandie hurriedly added her cup to the other used ones and joined him as he headed toward the door. "I know what you mean," she said. Glancing back, she told Liza, "Would you please keep Snowball shut up in here and tell the others he is not to go outside without me?"

"Sho' 'nuff will, Missy 'Manda," Liza replied, smiling at her as she bent to open the oven.

When Mandie and Joe got to the parlor, they found Mrs. Taft sitting by the fire in the fireplace. She looked up as they came into the room.

"My, you two are up early," Mrs. Taft said.

"Yes, ma'am," Mandie and Joe both replied.

The two sat down near Mrs. Taft, and Mandie explained about Snowball finally coming home.

"Well, I'm glad he came back, but, Amanda, please keep that cat shut up somewhere so he can't run off again," her grandmother replied.

"He's staying in the kitchen for the time being," Mandie said and then, looking at her grandmother, asked, "You are up awfully early, aren't you?"

Mrs. Taft cleared her throat and said, "Well, yes, I suppose so, but I had some notes to write that I want to go in the mail today so that I can make plans for the summer."

"Notes about summer plans, Grandmother?" Mandie asked.

"Why, yes, I thought I'd ask Senator Morton to get together with us," she explained. "And I wrote the Pattons. We could make a trip to Charleston to the beach and see them this summer."

"Senator Morton and the Pattons," Mandie repeated and glanced at Joe. He nodded as though reading her mind, and she continued, "Grandmother, I hope you are not including me, because Joe is coming home for the summer vacation from college this year, and we want to plan something."

"Yes, I know he will be home. His mother has already told me," Mrs. Taft replied. "And of course we want to include Joe in any plans we make." She looked at Joe and smiled.

Joe smiled back and said, "Thank you for thinking of me, Mrs. Taft."

Mandie was upset by her grandmother's plans but tried hard not to show it. "Does my mother know what you are planning? I mean, is she going to be involved, too?" she asked.

"Of course, your mother always goes along with whatever plans I make," Mrs. Taft replied.

Joe spoke up. "I'm not sure what plans I will make yet for the summer. Have you discussed your plans with my mother?"

Mrs. Taft looked at him and smiled as she said, "Your mother informed me that anything I wanted to plan would be fine with her, and of course she meant you, too."

Joe scratched his unruly brown hair and said, "But she doesn't know what plans I have for the summer because we haven't discussed them yet."

Mandie cleared her throat and tried to steady her voice as she spoke. "Grandmother, I am planning to visit my Cherokee kinpeople this summer. I haven't mentioned this to my mother, but I'm sure she will agree. So before you make any definite commitments with Senator Morton and the Pattons, maybe we'd better all get together and discuss this summer's activities." She held her breath, waiting for her grandmother to explode. Much to her surprise, Mrs. Taft didn't seem to have an answer to that.

Finally Mrs. Taft said, "Yes, we can all discuss this sometime today, I hope."

Mrs. Woodard and Elizabeth came into the parlor then. Mandie held her breath and hoped her grandmother did not want to have that discussion right now. She was hungry, and breakfast would be ready soon. Besides, she planned to talk privately with her mother first.

"Good morning," Elizabeth greeted everyone as she took a seat by the fire. "I'm sure glad to see the sun out this morning."

As greetings were exchanged, Mrs. Woodard also sat down, glanced at Joe, and said, "Yes, that sunshine is welcome, especially with the doctor having to make a call up the mountain this morning."

"Dad is already out and gone?" Joe asked his mother.

"Yes, it was time for more medicine for old Mr. Hanback, and your father decided this morning would be a good time to go," Mrs. Woodard said. "He'll be back in time for the noon meal."

"I'm glad Mr. Shaw didn't go with him, then, because he and I are going to cover the rose arbor after breakfast," Joe told her. Smiling, he added, "If it rains again we'll have a roof to stand under to watch that old house down by the creek."

The three ladies looked at him and shook their heads. Mrs. Woodard said, "I don't understand what the fascination is about that old place. Why, it's nothing but a barn, from what I remember."

"But, Mother, someone is staying in it, no matter how run-down the house is, and whoever it is certainly tries not to be seen by anyone," Joe said. He glanced at Mandie with a big grin and added, "It may be an outlaw, for all we know."

"Joe! I hope not," Elizabeth Shaw spoke quickly.

"Then it could be dangerous for you young people to snoop around down there," Mrs. Taft said, looking at Elizabeth.

"They've been cautioned not to go all the way to the house and especially not to go down that way alone," Elizabeth explained.

In an effort to turn the conversation away from the old house, Mandie explained to her mother and Mrs. Woodard that Snowball had returned home the night before.

"He's confined to the kitchen right now with notice that no one is to let him out," Joe added.

"I'm glad he came home," Elizabeth said.

"Yes, indeed, he's like one of the family," Mrs. Woodard added, smiling at Mandie.

John Shaw came to the parlor doorway then and informed them, "I believe breakfast is ready if you ladies are ready."

As soon as breakfast was over, John Shaw took Joe out to the barn with him to sort out the wood for the arbor. Mandie followed.

As she stood there, looking at the rough lumber her uncle was laying out, she asked, "Uncle John, that's going to look awfully tacky, isn't it—all that unfinished lumber on top of the rose arbor?"

John Shaw laughed and said, "It won't look that way when we get through with it. We're going to saw some of the good pieces, and after it's all attached to the arbor, we'll paint it."

"But if it rains again you won't be able to paint the wood in the rain," Mandie reminded him.

John Shaw straightened up to look at her and said, "Joe and I are going to do this real fast-like before it rains again so we can get the paint on before the wood gets wet. The sky looks bright and clear today, so I believe we have at least today to do this without rain."

Mandie decided to talk to her uncle about her summer plans while her grandmother was not around. She watched him and Joe laying out a pile of wood to be used and then finally spoke. "Uncle John, I would like to go visit my Cherokee kinpeople this summer. I haven't been out there in a long time."

John Shaw straightened up once more to look at her and said, "That is a good suggestion for the summer. I'd like to go visit them myself. My uncle is getting rather old now. When would you like to go?"

Mandie turned to grin at Joe. "As soon as school is out. And Joe will be coming home for the summer vacation and wants to go with us."

"Now, you've come up with some nice plans for the summer, Amanda," John Shaw said, smiling at Joe.

"And I've already mentioned this to Celia, and if her mother doesn't have something else planned, she would like to go with us," Mandie added.

"That's fine," Uncle John answered.

"However, we have some obstacles to overcome," Mandie warned with a big grin.

"We do?" her uncle questioned.

"Yes, in the form of my grandmother. She has been writing notes to Senator Morton and to the Pattons about possible vacation plans, without even asking anyone else," Mandie said with a loud moan.

"That sounds like her," John Shaw replied. "But let's look at it this way. This is your and Joe's vacation, so I'd say it's up to you two to decide what we will be doing. The rest of us are free to travel at other times, while y'all have to be in school and such."

"Thank you, Uncle John, for understanding," Mandie said. "But please tell me how we get around Grandmother and her plans."

"Hmmm!" John Shaw cleared his throat. "I think if you'll just leave that to me, I'll take care of it."

Mandie's face lit up in a big grin as she looked at Joe and said, "I knew I should include Uncle John in our plans. He's the only one who will stand up to my grandmother."

"Now, Amanda," Uncle John teased her, "you make me sound like I'm hard to get along with."

"No, you just have the gumption to stand up and be heard," Mandie replied.

"All right, I'm standing up now, and since you insisted on coming along with us, Amanda, I suggest you grab a piece of that lumber, and Joe and I will get the rest and we'll get started on this thing."

They carried the lumber and nails and hammers down to the old arbor. John Shaw checked it to be sure it was strong enough to stand the weight on the top. Then, satisfied with that, he began figuring how they would attach the additional boards.

Mandie looked around the area. There were jonquils up around the edge of the clearing, and sticky rosebushes not yet in bloom more or less surrounded the structure. Someone had made a low wall of rocks around the clearing, and that would be a comfortable place to sit. Glancing down the hill, she could see the old house and knew they had found the proper spot for their surveillance.

"This is nice, Uncle John," she told him as she watched.

"It hasn't exactly been kept up the last few years since we built the summer house in the front yard. Everyone seems to go there instead of here to sit outdoors for fresh air and sunshine," he replied.

Mandie turned slightly and saw Liza coming down the hill toward them, carrying Snowball. Now, why had she taken the cat out of the kitchen?

"Liza, what are you doing with Snowball?" she asked when the girl caught up with them.

"Dis heah cat, he ain't got no sandbox in de kitchen, so Aunt Lou, she say for me to put on his leash and take him outside," Liza explained, setting the cat down at the end of his leash, which she held.

"Oh, Liza!" Mandie exclaimed. "I'm sorry I didn't even think about things like that. Thank you for bringing him to me." She took the end of the red leash from the girl.

"I sees we gwine have a rainproof place to spy on dat house now, ain't we?" Liza said, watching John Shaw and Joe work on the cover.

"Yes, and I suppose by the time we get it all

done, we'll suddenly find out who's in that old house and we won't need it then," Joe told her with a big grin, picking up some nails and a hammer.

"Well, we can always use this as a place to sit," Mandie told him.

"Y'all gwine come stay home heah fo' the summer vacation?" Liza asked.

Mandie quickly looked at the girl and came up with a new idea. "Liza, we are probably going to visit my Cherokee kinpeople," she said. "How would you like to go with us?"

"And hafta eat owl stew and sech?" Liza asked, rolling her eyes.

"No, you don't have to eat owl stew. The Cherokee people cook lots of things that we eat, too," Mandie said, grinning at her. "Wouldn't you like to have a vacation with us?"

"I ain't sho' Aunt Lou 'llow dat," Liza mumbled indecisively.

John Shaw stopped his hammering and said, "Now, Liza, if you want to go with us, I'm sure it will be all right with Aunt Lou. With all of us gone she won't have a lot of work to do."

"Hmmm!" Liza still mumbled and traced a mark in the wet dirt with the toe of her shoe. "Mebbe, mebbe not. I'll let you know."

Everyone smiled and then Liza said, "I'se got to git back and he'p wit the cookin' fo' dinner," Liza said, turning to go back up the hill. Then looking back she said, "Missy 'Manda, don't let dat cat run away again."

"Mandie!" Joe exclaimed.

Mandie looked to see why he was being so loud.

"You might have made a big mistake," Joe told her. "If Liza goes back to the house and tells everyone you have invited her to go with you to visit your

Cherokee kinpeople, word is certainly going to get back to Mrs. Taft."

"Oh, you're right, Joe," Mandie said, picking up Snowball. "I'll go catch Liza and ask her not to mention it." She started to run up the hill.

"Amanda!" John Shaw called to her. She stopped and looked back. "I don't want you to be afraid of what your grandmother might hear or think. This is your vacation we're talking about, so don't worry about Liza telling everyone. In fact, that might be the best way for your grandmother to realize you have definite plans of your own."

Mandie smiled and went back down to the arbor. "Thank you, Uncle John," she said. "We'll just wait and see what happens."

Mandie knew her grandmother could be bossy and that most people gave in to her wishes, but John Shaw was not one of those. And she had her uncle strongly by her side. This was going to be an interesting problem, but she knew that somehow it would be solved.

Chapter 7 / Preparing

The cover over the rose arbor was finished and painted by the time Liza came to get them for the noonday meal. Mandie had helped by picking up nails, handing up tools as Joe and John Shaw stood on ladders, and then cleaning up the debris. Snowball, much to his dislike, had his leash looped around a post and had to stay right there with his mistress. He greeted Liza with loud meows.

"I knows, I knows," Liza told him as she walked up. "You wants loose, but I tells you you cain't get loose." She stooped to rub his head.

"I suppose it's eating time?" Joe asked with a grin.

"Dat's right. Aunt Lou sent me to tell y'all to git cleaned up 'cause de food gwine be on de table soon, and she say come right now," the girl replied.

"She timed it just right. We are finished with everything," John Shaw said, stepping back to look at their work.

"Liza, if you will take charge of Snowball, I'll help Uncle John and Joe take things back to the barn," Mandie said. "And please don't let him get loose."

"I'll take him right back to de kitchen. He'll like dat 'cause de food's ready and smellin' good," Liza said, unhooking the leash from the post and starting back up the hill with Snowball walking at the end of it.

Mandie glanced down the hill at the old house plainly in view from the rose arbor. "This is going to be the perfect place to watch from," she said.

"Provided we stay at least half hidden behind the bushes around this," Joe remarked, pointing to the shrubbery bushes growing at the edge of the arbor.

Then Mandie remembered the tunnel. "I don't think we have to check out the exit from the tunnel, Joe, because this is much better," she said, her hands full of scraps from the wood.

"I agree," Joe replied, pulling down the ladder he had been standing on to put finishing touches on the paint.

"This also made a big improvement in our yard," John Shaw remarked. He gathered up the tools.

As they all started back up the hill, Mandie said, "I don't know when Grandmother is planning on doing it, but she said this morning we could all discuss our plans for the summer. I just wanted to give you warning."

"Don't worry about it, my little blue eyes," John Shaw replied with a smile. "I learned long ago how to do battle with that grandmother of yours. We'll win this one."

"I hope so," Mandie replied.

After they left everything in the barn, they went in through the back door of the house to let Aunt Lou know they had returned. She gave them time to go upstairs and clean up and then announced the noonday meal just as the three of them joined the ladies in the parlor.

"I'm glad we didn't have time to talk in the parlor, so Grandmother couldn't bring up the subject of summer plans," Mandie whispered to Joe as they followed the adults into the dining room.

There was the sound of the front door opening and closing, and they looked back down the hallway to see Dr. Woodard coming in.

"You're just in time to eat," Mandie called to him.

"I'll join y'all just as soon as I clean up," the doctor replied, hurrying to the staircase.

Everyone else heard his reply as they went into the dining room. They sat at the table and waited for him to come in. When Dr. Woodard took his seat, the conversation was concerning patients he had stopped by to see on his way back.

"I don't think Grandmother will have an opportunity to bring up the subject of summer vacation anytime soon," Mandie whispered to Joe.

"No, my dad is a big talker once he gets started, especially about his patients," Joe agreed. "But that's good so we can eat in peace and not worry about plans." He grinned at Mandie.

Mandie noticed her grandmother was not talking very much. She decided maybe the lady just didn't want to discuss anything about summer vacation but was secretly making plans anyway. Then she wondered if her uncle John would broach the subject himself, but he was busy talking about their work on the old rose arbor.

Then when the meal was over, Elizabeth pushed back her chair and asked, "Would everyone be interested in going for a drive around town to get some fresh air in this wonderful sunshine we have today?"

As her mother looked around the table, Mandie shook her head. She wanted to stay home and relax. Then she caught Joe shaking his head also.

"All right, we'll go as soon as Abraham can hitch up the rig and we freshen up a little," Elizabeth said,

in response to the agreement that went around the
table. Then she walked by Mandie and Joe and said,
"You two don't have to go if you don't want to."

"Thanks, Mother," Mandie said as Elizabeth
walked on with the other ladies. Turning to Joe,
Mandie said, "Come on. Let's go sit in the parlor
until everyone leaves and then we can go watch the
old house. Maybe the paint on the arbor will be dry
by then."

"Maybe," Joe replied as he followed her down
the hallway to the parlor.

The adults had only been gone a few minutes,
and Mandie and Joe were getting ready to go outside, when Liza came to the parlor.

"Guess whut?" she said, smiling. "Y'all got mo'
company."

"More company? Who is it, Liza?" Mandie asked
eagerly.

"It be dat Injun man and dat man whut lives in
yo' daddy's house," Liza replied.

"Oh, where are they?" Mandie asked, excitedly
getting up from her chair.

"Dey puttin' de wagon in de barn. Ain't been to
de door yet but I seed 'em," Liza explained.

"Come on," Mandie told Joe as she rushed out
of the room.

Joe followed her to the kitchen, where the two
men were just coming in the back door.

"Uncle Ned!" Mandie exclaimed as she hurried
to shake his hand. The tall old Indian bent to give her
a hug. "And Mr. Jacob!" Mandie continued her
greetings as she reached for his hand. The big, burly
gray-haired man squeezed hers in reply.

"It's been so long since I saw you I thought I'd
come with Uncle Ned here when he stopped by and

told me he was coming over here," Mr. Jacob Smith told her.

Turning to Joe, Mr. Smith said with a chuckle, "Glad to see you managed to get away from that college."

"Yes, sir, I have to once in a while. I'm glad you came because I won't be home except long enough to get my things and go back to school. We're staying here until then," Joe replied.

Uncle Ned was standing by, watching and listening. "Believe you grow since I saw you," he said.

"Yes, sir, Uncle Ned, I'm sure I have because my pants are getting too short," Joe answered with a laugh.

Aunt Lou had been standing at the sink, observing. She spoke up, "Y'all jes' go sit at de table and I brings you some dinner. Everybody else done finished and gone out, but we still got food here." She pointed to the food on the sideboard she and Liza had brought from the dining room.

The men hesitated a moment and Mandie said, "Come on, sit down and eat. Mother and Uncle John and the others have gone for a drive but they'll be back soon." She walked over to the cupboard and began getting down dishes. Liza came to help.

While the men ate, Mandie and Joe drank coffee. Aunt Lou and Liza sat down by the cookstove where Snowball was eating from a plate on the floor.

"Is everything all right at my father's house?" Mandie asked.

"Just fine," Jacob Smith replied between bites of green beans. "That was why I wanted to see you, just to let you know everything is all right. I've made some repairs to the shutters and the front porch and I've painted the inside of the house."

"Oh, thank you, Mr. Jacob," Mandie said. "I'm

so glad I found you to live in the house and take care of it for me. I wouldn't want just anybody staying there. And did you finally get your own chickens so you don't have to buy eggs from the neighbors?"

"The pen is full of chickens and I have two hogs in the back of the barnyard. I'm also getting some cows and another horse," he told her. "In fact, the place is pretty well full of animals."

Turning to Uncle Ned, Mandie asked, "How is Sallie? And Morning Star?"

The old man smiled at her and said, "Sallie want Papoose come visit when summer get here."

Mandie grinned and looked at Joe as she replied, "Joe and I both are coming to visit when school is out. I want to see all my Cherokee kinpeople over in Deep Creek, but I'd rather stay at your house."

"I saw that missionary fellow who started the Cherokee school at the store the other day. He was asking about you, whether I had heard from you or not," Mr. Smith said.

"Riley O'Neal," Mandie said. "So he is still there. I thought maybe he would go back home to Boston."

"No, don't believe he'll be going back north anytime soon," Mr. Smith said. "He's really doing a good job with the Cherokee children. And their mamas and papas have finally decided he is their friend."

"I'm glad for him," Mandie said. "He seemed so sincere about getting the school started, and I was afraid the Cherokee people would never accept him."

Uncle Ned looked at Mandie and asked, "What Papoose been doing now?"

Mandie smiled and began relating the news regarding the old house down by the creek. "It's all a mystery right now, but I'm going to solve it before I go back to school," she said. Then, looking at Joe, she added, "And Joe is going to help me."

"She means I am just following along," Joe said, grinning.

"Man live there go away many years ago," Uncle Ned told them.

"You knew the man, Uncle Ned?" Mandie asked.

Uncle Ned smiled and replied, "Yes, when Morning Star and I stay here with John Shaw's papa."

"Oh, I had forgotten about y'all living with my grandparents way back then," Mandie said. "You don't think it could be that man who is staying down at the old house? Maybe he came back."

Uncle Ned shook his head and said, "Hear man went to happy hunting ground after he leave here."

"If that man died, who owns the place now, Uncle Ned?" Joe asked.

"Nobody," the old man replied.

"Might be something your uncle would want to buy since it joins his property," Jacob Smith said.

"I'll tell him," Mandie said.

"He'd probably have trouble tracing the ownership since the man is dead. There might be relatives who would be the owners now," Joe suggested.

Mandie gave him a big smile and said, "You really are going to turn into a lawyer, aren't you?"

Joe grinned back and said, "Well, we've been studying property laws at my school."

"That would be a good field to get into," Jacob Smith told him.

Uncle Ned shook his head and said sadly, "Property law no good for Cherokee people."

Mandie quickly reached across the table to squeeze the old man's hand. With tears in her eyes she told him, "Uncle Ned, you know what I'm going to do? I'm going to ask Uncle John to buy that piece of property down there and give it to you and Morning Star." Her voice trembled slightly as she thought about the dishonesty that had displaced her Cherokee ancestors from their very own land.

"But what we do with it?" Uncle Ned asked, squeezing her hand back. "We have house already."

"Oh, that house down there is no good, Uncle Ned," Mandie said with a little laugh. "It needs to be torn down and a new one built. Uncle John could build a new house for you, and then you and Morning Star and Sallie could come back here to live."

"Big God bless you, Papoose, but we cannot come here to live," the old man said, smiling at her. "We live at Deep Creek."

"But you and Morning Star lived here before with my grandparents," Mandie argued. "I know you and I are not blood related, and I do have lots of Cherokee kinpeople, real ones, but Uncle Ned, I love you and Morning Star so much more than I do them."

"Love Jim Shaw's Papoose," Uncle Ned replied, the nearest to tears she had ever seen him. "We love you, too."

"Anyhow," Mandie said, withdrawing her hand in order to take a sip of her coffee. "I'm going to ask Uncle John about buying that property and putting up a new house. Someday you and Morning Star may want it."

Silence had fallen across the room as everyone in it had listened to the conversation. Then Joe spoke up. "You know, Mandie, that might be a good learning experience for me to get involved in. You ask your uncle about it and if he's interested I'll volunteer to help him out."

Everyone laughed. "Help him out with what, Joe?" Mandie asked.

"Whatever needs to be done," Joe replied. "I know how to check property records in the courthouse and I also know how to use a hammer and a saw."

"Well, now, that certainly makes you qualified," Jacob Smith said. "Any which way you're needed."

When the room had become quiet again, Uncle Ned spoke. "Someday Joe will be a great lawyer. He has desire and ability, and with both there will be much success."

The room was very quiet after that remark and then suddenly Mandie clapped her hands and said, "And I want to be the first to congratulate Joe Woodard on a great future. I know him well enough to know that he will succeed at whatever he wishes to do." She felt her face grow warm with a blush as she dropped her eyes and quickly picked up her cup to sip her coffee.

"Amen!" came from Jacob Smith.

"Yes!" Uncle Ned followed.

Even Aunt Lou and Liza, listening to the conversation from their places by the stove, clapped their hands.

"Mandie, what are you trying to do? Embarrass me?" Joe exclaimed, dropping his eyes and not looking at anyone.

At that very moment John Shaw walked into the kitchen. "Embarrass you, Joe Woodard? Impossible!" and then he saw Uncle Ned and Jacob Smith. He stepped forward to shake hands. "How wonderful to find y'all here," he told them.

Aunt Lou came hurrying across the room with another cup and saucer, stopped at the stove to fill it with hot coffee, then brought it to the table and set it down.

John Shaw said, "Thank you, Aunt Lou," as he

pulled out a chair and sat down. "And, Jacob, how are things at Charley Gap?"

"Fine, just fine. I just told Miss Amanda I had made a few minor repairs on her house," he replied and explained what they were.

Mandie could hardly wait for the three men to get finished with their conversation, and she took their first break to put in her news. "Uncle John, did you know the man who owned that old house down by the creek died after he left here? Uncle Ned knew him and just told us."

John Shaw looked at Uncle Ned and asked, "So he died? Do you know if he had any relatives, if there was anyone who inherited the property?"

Uncle Ned shook his head and said, "Do not know of any. He live alone way over in Buncombe County, this McCampbell man. Friend neighbor tell me he die alone, church bury him, sad no kin-people."

"Yes, that is sad," John Shaw said. "I think I'll have my lawyer look into this, find out who, if anybody, owns the property now and whether it can be bought with a clear title."

Mandie grinned at her uncle. "I knew you would want to do that," she said.

"Maybe I could help," Joe offered. "I've learned how to look up property records, and the courthouse is right here in Franklin, and I will be here until the end of next week."

John Shaw looked at Joe and smiled. "Sure, Joe, you and Amanda go down to the courthouse and find the record, see if Mr. McCampbell ever sold the property, and if so, to whom."

"Thank you, sir, this will be a good learning experience for me," Joe told him.

"Don't forget, first we have to solve the mystery

of who is staying in that house," Mandie reminded him. "It could be somebody who has bought it."

"You're right, Amanda," John Shaw said. "It could have been sold."

"Well, then, let's work real fast on that mystery so I will still have time to go to the courthouse," Joe said with a disappointed look.

"If we are going to work that fast, we may have to sleep all day and stay up all night to watch that house because the light is only seen at night," Mandie told him.

"It's only seen at night because it's dark then. There may be a light inside in the daytime that we can't see in the light of day," Joe reminded her. "Besides, whoever is in there may come outside during the day sometime or other."

John Shaw stood up and said, "Uncle Ned, Jacob—the ladies are in the parlor. Suppose we join them."

As soon as the three men left the kitchen, Liza asked Mandie excitedly, "Kin I he'p watch if y'all watch at night, 'cause I don't be havin' to work at night?" She came over to the table.

"We'll have to decide exactly what we are going to do first, Liza," Mandie said. "But of course you can come with us anytime Aunt Lou says you can."

Aunt Lou rose from her chair and said, "Liza, right now we needs to finish cleaning up dis heah kitchen fo' it git time to cook supper."

"Yessum, Aunt Lou, I'll hurry," Liza said, rushing around taking the dirty dishes from the table and carrying them to the sink.

Mandie told Joe, "Since the sun has been shining today, it ought to be clear tonight and a little warmer without all that rain. Do you want to go sit in the arbor after we have supper? It'll be dark by then."

"Sure, if you'll agree to at least walk down to the courthouse sometime tomorrow. We don't have to start looking for records. We can just walk in and see where everything is kept," Joe said, smiling.

"Have you never been in the courthouse?" Mandie asked.

"No, this one is for Macon County, here," Joe said. "Since I live in Swain County, our courthouse is in Bryson City. Remember when we went to court about your father's house?"

"I've been in this one here one time," Mandie said. "It has indoor bathrooms, one for the ladies and one for the men, and it's all marble with fancy curlicues everywhere."

Aunt Lou stopped in the middle of the floor and said, "Now, my chile, what a subject for a young lady to discuss. Bathrooms, indeed!"

"Oh, Aunt Lou," Mandie exclaimed, blushing in spite of herself. She and Joe had always talked about everything and thought nothing of it. But now Aunt Lou was reminding her that she was a young lady and should act ladylike. Then, smiling, Mandie said, "Aunt Lou, I do believe you have been talking to Miss Prudence. She's always telling us the young ladies in her school should act like young ladies. But I'm home now and this is a holiday, so I can just be plain old me."

Aunt Lou sighed, walked over to the stove, and said, "Someday, my chile, you gwine hafta grow up."

"Hafta grow up," Liza repeated as she picked up more dishes. "Dat's whut Aunt Lou always tellin' me, and I ain't sho' I wants to grow up. Sounds like a lot of trouble to me, rememberin' all dem things."

Mandie and Joe both laughed and stood up.

"Come on, Joe, let's go to the parlor," Mandie said. "My grandmother may be discussing plans, and we need to know what's said."

"We sure do," Joe agreed.

As the two started for the door, Mandie looked back at Aunt Lou and said, "I'll try to remember, Aunt Lou."

Aunt Lou paused to smile at her.

Mandie secretly agreed with Liza. She wasn't sure she wanted to grow up and be a young lady. She might not have the opportunity to solve mysteries then, especially since she would not be able to do any unladylike things that might be necessary.

"Oh well!" Mandie whispered to herself.

Chapter 8 / Aunt Lou's Suggestion

Everyone sat in the parlor that night after supper and discussed everything from the weather to the upcoming dinner party, but no mention was made of plans for the summer. Mandie stayed right there to be sure her grandmother didn't bring up the subject of summer vacation, and when Mrs. Taft finally declared she was tired and would like to retire, Mandie blew out a breath of relief.

"Now we can go to the arbor and watch that house," Mandie whispered to Joe as Mrs. Taft left the parlor.

"All right," Joe agreed.

Mandie made motions to Uncle John, who was sitting nearest to them, that they were going outside. He nodded and smiled. Everyone else was so involved in conversation that they didn't notice when the two quietly left the room.

However, someone else was waiting for them. As soon as they stepped into the hallway, Liza appeared from the direction of the kitchen and said, "Lawsy mercy, Missy 'Manda, thought y'all never was goin' to go to dat arbor place. I been waitin' ever since we cleaned up de kitchen. We needs to git goin' so's we kin have time to sleep a little bit tonight."

Mandie smiled at the girl and said, "Sorry, Liza,

but I had to wait until my grandmother went to bed to be sure she didn't bring up plans for the summer." She and Joe walked down toward the back door. Liza followed.

"Besides, we didn't know you were waiting. You didn't let us know," Joe added.

"All right, den, next time I let you know," Liza replied.

"Is Snowball still in the kitchen?" Mandie asked as she came to the door.

"Last time I was in dere he be dere," Liza assured her. "And I was de onliest one left in dere, so I sho' ain't gwine let him out."

The moon was shining through the new leaves of the trees and lighted the way down to the rose arbor. Then they discovered if they sat inside the arbor they would be in shadows but could see the old house down the hill by the light of the moon.

They sat on the plank bench that ran around the interior and waited. For a while no one spoke as they kept their eyes toward the old house. Finally Liza grew impatient and said, "Missy 'Manda, don't y'all be thinkin' we jes' oughta walk on down a piece so's we kin see better?"

"I suppose we could, but we'll have to be awfully quiet and careful to stay behind bushes," Mandie warned as they stood up.

"And please watch where y'all step," Joe added. "The pathway is steep and uneven. I don't think I could pick up two girls at one time." He laughed.

"I can see de path all right anyhow," Liza said.

"I'll be careful," Mandie said, following Joe as he led the way.

They were almost at the boundary line when Mandie held up her hand and whispered, "I think this is far enough." She moved behind a bush.

Joe and Liza joined her, and they kept peeping around the bush to look at the old house as they stood there.

Time seemed to drag with nothing happening. Mandie became tired of standing and looked around. "Is there some place we could sit down for a while?" she asked.

"There's a rock here on the other side of me," Joe said, pointing to his left. "It may be wet and dirty, though."

Suddenly Liza squealed, "Lookie, lookie! Dere's a light down dere!"

Mandie looked at the old house. Sure enough, there was a faint light showing through a crack in the shutters. She held her breath in excitement.

"Yes, there's a light, but what do we do now that we've seen it?" Joe quickly asked.

Mandie thought for a moment and then said, "I suppose there's nothing we can do unless we just walk down there and knock on the door." She looked at Joe.

"Mandie, I don't think that would be safe. Remember your uncle cautioned us about who might possibly be in that old house?" Joe replied.

"I could go knock on dat do' and y'all could jes' watch out fo' me," Liza offered. "And if'n it be a bad man I kin run pritty good."

"No, Liza, I'm afraid something might happen to you down there," Mandie told her.

"Mandie, I think the best thing we can do is go to the courthouse tomorrow and find out who the owner is," Joe suggested. "And then we could find out somehow or other whether that's the owner inside."

Mandie sighed and said, "Yes, I suppose we do need to know who owns the old house."

"But tomorrow de light may git away somewhere and not come back anymore," Liza protested.

"I'm sorry, Liza, but we just can't go down there tonight," Mandie said. "Maybe when we tell Uncle John about seeing the light, he will want to go with us and knock on the door tomorrow."

They returned to the house and found all the adults still in the parlor. Stopping at the door, Mandie got John Shaw's attention and motioned for him to come out into the hallway.

"What is it, my little blue eyes?" Uncle John asked as he stepped out of the room.

"The light! We saw the light just now," Mandie quickly told him. "And we didn't know what to do about it—"

John interrupted with a laugh and said, "There's nothing you can do about it, I'm afraid, because we have no idea who is holed up in there. However, you can still watch for whoever it is to come outside. Then you could find out what kind of a person is staying there."

"Do you mean it's all right if we run down there and speak to whoever it is if we see them come out of the house?" Mandie asked.

"Oh no, don't do that," John Shaw replied. "You just let me know if you see anyone and I'll handle it from there."

"And if you go down there can we go with you?" Joe asked.

"I woulda went down dere jes' now but Missy 'Manda, she wouldn't let me," Liza mumbled.

John turned to Liza and said, "No, you are also forbidden to go down there because of possible danger." Looking back at Mandie, he asked, "Was it just a faint light showing through the shutters, or a stronger light?"

"A very faint light, Uncle John, almost so faint we couldn't see it," Mandie told him.

"Probably candlelight," he decided. "I just hope whoever is in there doesn't catch the place on fire. It could cross the line onto our property."

Mandie, Joe, and Liza all gasped at the same time.

"Then, Uncle John, I think we'd better hurry up and find out what's going on in that house," Mandie decided.

"Yes, I agree, but it's a problem not knowing who's inside."

"Sir, Mandie and I agreed we'd go to the court-house tomorrow and check the records to find out who owns the house, and then maybe we could just walk up, knock on the door, and say, 'Howdy, Mr. Jones, or whoever it is, we are your neighbors.' At least we'd have the owner's name."

John Shaw smiled at Joe and said, "Y'all go ahead and look up the property records and then we'll talk about what to do next."

"First thing in the morning," Mandie promised as John Shaw went back inside the parlor.

"Did y'all be a-knowin' dere's chocolate cake left from suppuh?" Liza asked with a big grin, practically dancing around the hall in her excitement.

"Where?" Joe quickly asked.

"Come on, let's find it," Mandie decided, leading the way toward the kitchen door.

When they entered the kitchen, there was no one there except Snowball. He was so thrilled at seeing his mistress he began loudly meowing and rushed to rub around her ankles.

Mandie bent to pet his head. "I know all about you," she said. "You are being good thinking I'll let you out of here, aren't you?"

Liza hurried to the pie safe, took out the huge plate with part of a chocolate cake on it, and carried it to the table.

Joe went over to check the percolator on the stove. It seemed to be full of coffee.

Mandie got down cups and saucers and cake plates, while Liza brought silverware from the cupboard.

"Looks like we have everything we need," Mandie remarked as Liza began cutting the cake and Joe began filling the coffee cups.

Just as they got everything ready and sat down at the long table, the door opened and Aunt Lou came into the room. "I knowed y'all would come back lookin' fo' dat cake. Dat's why I left de pot full of coffee." She smiled at them.

"Aunt Lou, come join us," Mandie urged the old woman.

Liza jumped up, got a plate and cup for Aunt Lou, and brought them to the table. Joe poured her coffee for her.

Aunt Lou just stood there watching them. Finally she grinned and said, "Now, ain't dat all temptin', jes' so temptin' I jes' can't refuse." She sat down at the table.

Between bites of chocolate cake and sips of hot coffee, the young people told Aunt Lou about seeing the light.

"I knows dey must be somebody in dat house," the old woman said. "Mebbe dey po' people and hungry. I could fix a basket of food and axe Abraham to take it to dem, mebbe."

"Oh, Aunt Lou, that's a good idea," Mandie said, smiling at her. "Maybe I could go with Abraham."

"No, no, my chile. Mistuh John, he give orders dat nobody to go down dere," the old woman replied. "But now Abraham being an old man, it might be safe fo' him to jes' knock on de door, don't y'all think?" She looked around the table.

"That's right, but can't I just go with him?" Mandie insisted.

"No, no, you has to git permission from Mistuh John first," the old woman said. Then thoughtfully she added, "Tomorrow I fix de basket, whilst we have all de bakin' done and plenty to give away."

"I'll ask Uncle John, Aunt Lou, so will you wait to send Abraham until he tells me whether I can go or not?" Mandie said. "In fact, Uncle John is in the parlor. I'll go ask him right now." She stood up and started toward the door.

"Hurry back," Joe called to her.

But John Shaw was not in the parlor. When she looked inside and didn't see him, she asked her mother, who was talking to Mrs. Woodard and Mrs. Taft, "Mother, where did Uncle John go?"

"He and Doctor Woodard went upstairs to John's office to do some paper work," Elizabeth Shaw told her.

"Oh, shucks!" Mandie replied. The office was off limits at all times, and she knew she could not go up there and talk to him now. It would have to wait until tomorrow.

Mandie went back to the kitchen and told her friends, "So I won't be able to find out until tomorrow whether I can go with Abraham or not, Aunt Lou. Please don't send him until I talk to you."

"All right, my chile, we wait whilst you finds out," Aunt Lou agreed.

However, the next morning Mandie found out her uncle had left before daylight to go with Dr. Woodard to visit his patients. When she came into the kitchen, Aunt Lou was already there.

"Mistuh John done left," the old woman said, going about getting things ready for breakfast.

"Did he say when they would be back?" Mandie asked anxiously.

"My chile, he say dey got lots of people to see and don't wait on the noontime dinner fo' him," Aunt Lou replied.

Liza entered the kitchen, looking half asleep and yawning. She glanced around the room and asked, "I ain't late, is I, Aunt Lou?"

"No, not quite," Aunt Lou replied, turning to look at the girl.

Liza was trying to straighten out her long skirt and was pushing back her braided hair.

"Now, where 'bouts you been dis mawnin', Liza?" Aunt Lou asked.

"Dis mawnin' I ain't been nowhere, Aunt Lou, nowhere atall," she declared.

"Well, you sho' look like you slep' in dem clothes. In fact, dem's de same clothes what you had on last night," Aunt Lou continued looking at her, frowning. Then she suddenly asked, "Liza, didn't you git to bed last night?"

Liza immediately dropped her eyes and said, "Well, now, Aunt Lou, I git to bed—"

Aunt Lou interrupted, "You git to bed late and slep' in dem clothes or I ain't standin' heah. Liza, whut you been up to?"

Mandie was standing by listening to the conversation. She immediately figured that Liza had been back outside during the night, watching the old house. Turning to Liza with a big grin, she whispered in the girl's ear, "Liza, did you see another light in that house last night after we left?"

Liza looked shocked at the question, backed off, and didn't answer.

"Well, git a move on, now, Liza. We'se got to git breakfast ready," Aunt Lou said as she turned back to the pots on the stove.

Joe entered the kitchen then. Mandie quickly told him, "Come on, we're in the way of preparing breakfast here. Let's go outside." She started for the back door.

"Without even a cup of coffee?" Joe moaned as he followed.

"Y'all come back in five minutes and I'll have de coffee made," Aunt Lou told him.

Once they were out in the backyard, Joe asked, "Now, what is this all about?"

Mandie explained that her uncle had gone with Joe's father on his rounds and that Liza looked like she had stayed up all night and slept in her clothes.

"I'm pretty sure she went back outside to watch that house," Mandie said as they walked about the yard. "And I don't believe she saw a light or anything or she would have been anxious to tell me."

"She sure has developed a fascination for that old house," Joe remarked.

"And now I can't ask Uncle John about going with Abraham to take the basket of food until he comes back, and I don't know whether Aunt Lou will wait that long to send Abraham down there," Mandie complained.

"Don't you think it would be all right if I went with you and we followed Abraham down there? Sounds safe enough to me," he said.

"Probably," Mandie replied. "But I suppose I could tell my mother what I was doing. But then she might forbid it. I'll have to think about this. We aren't making any progress on this mystery."

"No, but tomorrow is Friday, and Celia will be

arriving then. Maybe she can help us find some way to solve it," Joe suggested.

"Yes, she will be getting here tomorrow, but I suppose Uncle John's restrictions will still apply, even with her here," Mandie said.

"Why don't we just walk down the hill to the arbor and take a look at the old house in the daylight?" Joe asked.

"Great idea, let's do," Mandie agreed.

Together they went down the hill and stopped at the rose arbor. The sun was shining on the old house, making it plainly visible. And at the moment they stopped, Mandie caught the motion of the door being quickly closed.

"Joe! Did you see that?" she asked excitedly.

"Sure did," Joe replied.

The two continued staring at the old house. Mandie held her breath, hoping the door would open and someone would come out.

"Oh, whoever that was probably saw us," Mandie said in a disappointed voice.

"And therefore they probably won't come out again," Joe agreed.

"We might as well give up and go back to get that cup of coffee," Mandie added.

"That's a good idea. I can think better with coffee," Joe said.

As they turned back up the hill, Mandie said, "We could eat breakfast and then come back. If whoever it was saw us, they'll know we are gone. We could go back down the other pathway where they wouldn't be expecting us and maybe we could see something from there. What do you think?"

"Yes, that's a bright idea."

"And, Joe, please help me remember to be sure Snowball is left in the kitchen and everyone knows he is not to be let out," Mandie said.

"Yes, he could spoil everything again," Joe agreed.

As they climbed back up the hill, Mandie thought about all kinds of possibilities as a solution to the secret of the old house. As Uncle John had suggested, there might be some kind of crook in there, or there could be someone sick, or lost.

"Don't forget you promised to go with me to the courthouse this morning," Joe reminded her as they reached the backyard.

"Oh, that's right," Mandie replied. "I suppose we'd better go to the courthouse first and then come back and go down there to look at that house."

"Yes, I'm anxious to find out who owns it now," Joe said.

"But we probably won't know them," Mandie said.

"Yes, but it might be a name that your uncle John would recognize," he answered.

"All right, I hope it won't take long," Mandie said as they walked up to the back porch.

Joe smiled at her and said, "Mandie, you're always in a hurry about everything. Slow down. You may breeze past something important someday without seeing it."

Mandie laughed and said, "I hope not."

As they entered the back hallway, Mandie thought about what Joe had said. Maybe she did move too fast sometimes, but then things had a way of moving so fast that she had to move fast to catch up with them.

She frowned as she said, "I'll just have to keep an eye out."

Chapter 9 / More Developments

When Mandie and Joe returned to the kitchen, they found Uncle Ned and Jacob Smith sitting at the table drinking coffee.

"Good morning," Mandie greeted the two men as she walked over to the table. Joe followed.

"Good morning, Papoose," Uncle Ned replied, smiling at her.

"Y'all are up and out early," Jacob Smith said.

Aunt Lou brought the percolator to the table and filled two empty cups sitting there. "Sit down and drink your coffee now," she told them.

"Thank you, Aunt Lou," Mandie replied as she and Joe sat down with the men. "We're not really early. Uncle John and Dr. Woodard left before we got up."

"My father always gets up earlier than anyone else," Joe said.

"We leave, too," the old Indian said as he sipped his coffee.

"Y'all are leaving? But you just got here yesterday," Mandie told him. "Why do you have to leave so soon?"

"Go over mountain to Yellow Hill, see friends, be back soon," Uncle Ned explained.

"When are y'all coming back? I'm only going to

be here till the end of next week and then I have to go back to school," Mandie reminded him.

"I'll see that he gets back in a day or two," Jacob Smith promised, smiling at Mandie.

"My father might have gone that way. He has some patients over that direction," Joe said. "You may catch up with him somewhere."

"Yes," Uncle Ned said. "People at Yellow Hill know doctor."

Mandie looked across the room at Aunt Lou by the stove and said, "Aunt Lou, with Uncle John gone already, I can't ask him to go with Abraham to take that basket of food to that old house. Would you please wait and send Abraham after Uncle John comes back so I can ask to go?"

"Well, now, my chile, I s'pose I could wait till early afternoon," the old woman replied. "But we shouldn't oughta wait too long 'cause whoever be in dat old house may be hungry."

Mandie grinned at her and said, "Oh, thank you, Aunt Lou. I'll ask him just as soon as he gets back. You see, if I ask my mother, then my grandmother might get involved in it and I don't think she would ever let me go."

"I understand, my chile," Aunt Lou replied. "I sho' does understand."

Liza came in the door from the dining room and announced, "I'se got de table all set now, Aunt Lou."

"Den go look in de parlor to see if Miz 'Lizbeth be in dere and ready fo' breakfast," Aunt Lou replied, stirring the contents of a pot.

"Yessum," Liza replied and went out the door to the hallway.

Mandie stood up and said, "I suppose we'd better go to the parlor so Mother will know where we are."

"Yes," Joe agreed as he, too, rose.

Uncle Ned and Jacob Smith followed them to the parlor, where Elizabeth Shaw, Mrs. Taft, and Mrs. Woodard were sitting. They met Liza in the doorway.

"Now that we are all together, let's have some breakfast," Elizabeth said, rising after she greeted the two men.

"And maybe we'll have a chance to discuss some plans for the summer," Mrs. Taft added.

Mandie held her breath when she heard that. As everyone went into the dining room and sat down at the table, she tried to listen to everything everyone said, which was mostly about nothing in particular except the dinner party planned for tomorrow night. And she noticed her mother and Mrs. Woodard did most of the talking. Mrs. Taft seemed to be deep in thought about something. Uncle Ned and Jacob Smith said very little, which was usual for them.

Then, as the meal was finished and everyone was leaving the dining room, Mandie stepped over to her mother and said, "Joe and I are going to the courthouse to look for the property owner's name for that old house down by the creek."

"Yes, dear, I believe I heard your uncle John say you all were going to do that for him," Elizabeth replied. "Just don't be gone too long, now."

"Yes, ma'am," Mandie replied.

She and Joe followed the men out into the backyard, where Jacob Smith and Uncle Ned got into the wagon to go over to the mountain, then she and Joe walked on downtown to the courthouse.

Joe looked around as they entered the building. "This is a nice courthouse," he remarked. "I'll go ask at the desk over there for directions to the property records." He walked on across the hallway to where a woman was sitting behind a desk. Mandie followed.

"We would like to find the records for that old house by the creek that joins Mr. John Shaw's property, please, ma'am," he told her.

"Oh, the McCampbell property," the woman said, looking up at him.

"Yes, ma'am, that's right. We heard Mr. Mc-Campbell died after he left here and we want to find out who owns the property now," Joe explained.

"I can tell you where to look up the records, but I can also tell you it has not been sold since Mr. McCampbell died," the woman replied. "It seems there are two distant cousins who are his closest surviving kin, and they are at each other's throats to get the property. May be a long court battle."

That news was unexpected, and Joe looked at Mandie.

"Do you know what lawyer is handling the case?" Joe asked the woman.

"Yes, that's Lawyer Tennyson and he's out of town on business until the first of the month," the woman told him.

"I see," Joe said, at a loss to know what to do now.

"Can you tell us the names of those two cousins who are fighting?" Mandie asked.

"No, but the clerk in that room over there can," the woman said, pointing across the hall to a room with the door standing open.

"Thank you," Joe quickly told her and started toward the room. "Thanks for asking that question. The information about the house was so unexpected I didn't quite know what to ask next."

They walked up to a long counter, where another woman was sitting sorting through papers. She didn't even look up when the two stopped in front of her.

After a minute or two Joe loudly cleared his throat and asked, "May we ask you a question, please?"

The woman still didn't look at them but continued with her paper work. Mandie looked at Joe and then leaned forward to place her hand across the counter as she said, "Ma'am, could you give us some information, please?"

Finally the woman looked up. She smiled, pointed to her ears, and pushed a piece of paper and a pencil across the counter to Mandie.

Mandie took it, frowned, looked at the woman again, and said in a whisper to Joe, "She must not be able to hear."

Joe nodded and said, "Yes, she wants you to write on the paper whatever you want to know."

When Mandie wrote the question and handed the woman the paper, the woman smiled and wrote back on the bottom of the sheet, *Dean White, New York, and George Littleton, Washington, D.C.*

Then Mandie had to write again and ask for the addresses to write to. The woman added that information and went back to her work.

Mandie and Joe looked over the paper together as they went back out into the hallway.

"Too bad I don't have more time at home. It'll take a while to get in touch with these people," Mandie said.

"Yes, and the attorney, too," Joe added.

"There is one thing we could ask that first lady we talked to," Mandie said, smiling. "Does she know if anyone is living in that old house?"

"You're right," Joe agreed.

They stopped back by the woman's desk and

inquired. She looked up at them in surprise and said, "No one is living there. The place is unfit for habitation. The land is what those two cousins are in a fight over. They know that house will have to be torn down."

"When did Mr. McCampbell die?" Joe asked.

"Oh, a long time ago. He hadn't lived here for about twenty years, I believe. He moved to Florida and died down there," the woman explained.

After thanking the clerk for the information, Mandie and Joe went outside and started walking back to the Shaws' house.

"I'd say we know one thing for sure," Mandie said, looking up at Joe as she tried to keep up with his long legs.

"What's that?" Joe asked.

"I don't believe that would be either of the two heirs living in that old house, so it must be a tramp," Mandie replied.

"Probably," Joe agreed. "So whoever is in there might be dangerous."

"But we can still go watch from the arbor," Mandie said.

When they got back to the house, they found Elizabeth, Mrs. Taft, and Mrs. Woodard had gone off in the rig. Aunt Lou didn't know where.

"Then Joe and I are going down to the arbor," Mandie told Aunt Lou.

"Just be sho' you back in time for de noonday meal 'cause Miz 'Lizbeth say dey be back den," the old woman reminded her.

"Yes, ma'am," Mandie replied, and looking at Joe, added, "Joe will be hungry by then."

"I certainly will," Joe agreed with a big grin.

Snowball jumped out of the woodbox and came running over to rub around his mistress's ankles.

Mandie stooped to rub his back. "You can't go with us, Snowball," she told the cat, then, looking up at Aunt Lou, she added, "Please don't let him out, Aunt Lou. I don't want him to follow me to the arbor."

"I sees he stay heah," Aunt Lou replied. "Jes' you don't be gwine close to dat house, my chile."

"We're only going to sit in the arbor," Mandie promised.

They watched the old house the rest of the morning, but there was no sign of anyone down there.

Liza came to get them when the noonday meal was ready. "And everybody else dun come back, too," she told them as the three walked up the hill.

"Everybody?" Mandie asked. "Uncle John and Dr. Woodard are back, too?"

Liza nodded her head and said, "Dey sho' is."

"Then I can ask about going with Abraham to take the basket," Mandie said, looking up at Joe.

"And I'll go with you and Abraham," Joe promised.

Later, when the meal was over, Mandie finally got a chance to ask her uncle, "Would it be all right if Joe and I went with Abraham to take a basket of food that Aunt Lou is sending down to that house?"

John Shaw looked down at her in surprise and asked, "Aunt Lou is sending food down there? Has someone been seen at the house? For all we know, there may not be anyone staying in it."

"Oh, Uncle John, you know how Aunt Lou is. She worries about other people being hungry," Mandie replied. "And suppose there is someone hungry in there?"

John Shaw smiled at her and said, "Well, I suppose it will be all right for you and Joe to go with Abraham, but, mind you, let him go first and do the knocking."

"Yes, sir," Mandie promised.

"But I don't imagine he will get any response," John Shaw continued. "If there is anyone in there, I wouldn't think they would want to be seen."

Then suddenly Mandie remembered the information they had obtained from the courthouse. "Oh, Uncle John, we forgot about this," she said. She pulled the paper out of her skirt pocket and handed it to him. "That's what we found out at the courthouse this morning."

"And we don't believe either of the relatives would be living in there," Joe added.

John glanced over the scribbling as the two explained what they had written down.

"So the house is still in Mr. McCampbell's name," John Shaw said. "You're right. I don't imagine either of these people would be living in that old shack. So it must be someone just holed up in there for some reason. I'm not sure you two ought to go down there."

"Oh, Uncle John, please? We'll stay away from the front door and let Abraham do the knocking like you said. Please," Mandie begged.

"If we had to we could always run away from there. There are plenty of trees and bushes nearby we could disappear into," Joe added.

John Shaw sighed and finally agreed, "All right, but I want to know as soon as you get back."

"Thank you, Uncle John," Mandie said.

"We'll come straight to you when we get back," Joe promised.

John Shaw went on toward the parlor to join the others. Mandie and Joe turned back toward the kitchen.

"Aunt Lou, we have permission to go with Abraham," Mandie quickly announced.

Aunt Lou stopped as she carried dishes to the sink and asked, "So now both of you has got permission, is dat right?"

"Uncle John said I could," Mandie replied.

"Well, now, whut about Joe dere?" Aunt Lou replied and then asked, "Did you ask your pa if you could go, too?"

Joe laughed and said, "Aunt Lou, I'm too old for that. My father gave me more freedom when I went off to college. He says I'm old enough to make my own decisions and that I will also have to live with the results if I make the wrong ones."

Aunt Lou looked at him for a moment, and Mandie was afraid she was going to doubt Joe's word. But then the woman smiled and said, "Jes' you be sho' nuthin' happens to my chile dere, understand?"

"Yes, ma'am, Aunt Lou, I'll look after Mandie," Joe promised. "Don't worry about her."

At that moment Liza came in the back door with Abraham. Aunt Lou pointed to the sideboard and said, "Abraham, I wants you to take dat basket of food down to dat old house by de creek."

"Yessum, Liza done tole me," he replied, walking over to pick up the basket.

"And dese heah chillen, dey gwine wid you. You jes' be sho' nuthin' happens to dem, understand?"

"Yessum, Aunt Lou, ain't nuthin' gwine happen to dem," Abraham replied.

"Den git outa heah and hurry back, now," she replied. "And, Liza, git in de dinin' room and git dem dishes in heah, real fast-like."

"Yessum," Liza replied, going toward the door to the dining room.

Abraham quickly went out the back door, with Mandie and Joe close behind him. They followed him down the hill, and just before they got to the creek Abraham stopped.

"Now, Mistuh John, he say y'all ain't gwine up to de do,' so y'all jes' stay in de yard when we gits dere, unnerstand?" he told them.

"All right, Abraham," Mandie agreed.

"Yes, sir, Abraham," Joe replied.

So when the three stepped into the yard of the old house, Mandie and Joe stopped near the steps and waited while Abraham went up and knocked on the door.

Mandie watched, her heart beating fast in expectation of what would happen. But even when Abraham knocked and knocked, louder and louder, there was not a sound in the house and no one opened the door. The old man scratched his head, stooped to set the basket in front of the door, and came back to join them in the yard.

"Ain't sho' dere's anybody in dat house," he told them and he started back up the hill. Mandie and Joe followed.

Mandie kept looking back just in case the door opened, but that didn't happen. Finally they reached the rose arbor.

"Why don't we sit here and watch for a while?" she asked Joe.

"Remember your uncle said he wanted to know as soon as we got back?" Joe reminded her.

"Oh, shucks!" Mandie exclaimed, continuing on up the hill. "Maybe if we hurry we can get back before someone gets that basket," she said, rushing. "Come on."

Joe caught up with her, and Abraham trailed behind.

"I've about decided there is no one in that

house," Joe said as they rushed up to the Shaws' house.

"We'll know if the basket disappears," Mandie said.

The two went down the hallway to the parlor, where John Shaw was sitting with the others. He looked up as they stopped in the doorway.

"We're back and nothing happened," Mandie quickly explained. "Abraham left the basket on the porch and we are going back to the arbor to watch."

"All right, but don't be gone too long," John Shaw said.

By the time the two got back to the rose arbor where they could see the old house, it was too late. The basket was gone.

"Oh, shucks!" Mandie exclaimed, almost in tears at the disappointment. "Somebody is in there, and they took the basket and we didn't get to see them."

"Come on over here and let's sit down," Joe told her, leading the way to the bench.

"Whoever is in there must have been watching, and as soon as we got out of sight they snatched the basket," Joe remarked as they sat looking down the hill. "Well, one good thing about it is the food was not wasted. Maybe whoever is in there was hungry, like Aunt Lou said."

"I would imagine Aunt Lou put enough food in that basket to last for days, so I don't suppose she will be sending another one down there anytime soon," Mandie said with a groan.

"No," Joe agreed.

At that moment Liza came hurrying down the hill toward them. When she finally got to the arbor, she asked, "What happened? Did dey come to de do'?"

Mandie explained what happened, then said, "And if I had not promised Uncle John to report right back to him, we might have seen them get the basket."

"Next time I goes wid y'all, and I stays right heah in de arbor and watches whilst y'all go report to Mistuh John," Liza replied.

"That's a good idea, Liza," Mandie agreed. "If Aunt Lou sends another basket we'll do just that— that is, if you can get away from Aunt Lou long enough."

"She let me go if you say so, Missy 'Manda," Liza replied.

Mandie thought about Liza's idea and then she remembered Celia was coming tomorrow. Maybe with her they could work something out for someone to keep watch while the others reported back to Uncle John.

She was positive someone was in the old house now, and she just had to find out who it was.

Chapter 10 / Celia Arrives

Friday morning the sun was shining brightly and the air was warmer. Mandie woke early and hurried to get dressed. She would be going with Uncle John to the depot after breakfast to meet Celia, Celia's mother, and her aunt Rebecca. She could hardly wait to tell her friend about what had been going on, and she was hoping Celia would agree to participate in the solution to the mystery.

Rushing down to the big kitchen, she found Uncle John and Joe already there, drinking coffee as usual. No matter how early she got up or how much she hurried, it was almost impossible to get there before her uncle. And that thought reminded her of those wonderful mornings she had spent with her father, Jim Shaw, in the kitchen before he died. John Shaw reminded her of her father so much, although his hair was dark and her father's had been red. Otherwise, they were almost like twin brothers not only in looks but in speech and mannerisms, too, even though John was older than his brother Jim.

Mandie paused just inside the door as these thoughts went through her head. Uncle John looked up from his cup of coffee and said, "Don't just stand there. I believe you are in bad need of a cup of coffee." He smiled at her.

Aunt Lou was over at the stove, and she hurriedly poured a cup of coffee from the percolator and brought it to the table for Mandie. "Heah, my child, you jes' sit down heah and wake up."

Mandie smiled at the woman and pulled out a chair and sat down beside Joe. "You are going to pick up Celia and Aunt Rebecca and Mrs. Hamilton, aren't you?" she reminded John.

"Yes, since Jason Bond is still away visiting over there in Swain County, I'll be the one to go meet the train," John Shaw replied. "And I suppose you are still planning to go with me, or will you be too busy watching that old house down there?" He grinned at her.

"Sure, I'm going with you, Uncle John. I've been waiting all week for this day to get here," Mandie replied, sipping the hot coffee. And as Aunt Lou came to refill John Shaw's coffee cup, Mandie asked her, "Are you planning on sending another basket of food down to the old house today?"

"Lawsy mercy, not today, my chile," Aunt Lou replied. "I puts enough food in dat one yesterday to feed a army. Mebbe tomorrow I send Abraham again. 'Sides, we got dat dinner party coming up tonight and dat's going to take a lot of time and a whole lot of food."

"Will you let me know when you do?" Mandie asked.

"I sho' will, my chile," Aunt Lou said, taking the percolator back to the stove.

Mandie glanced across the room and saw Snowball busily eating from a plate on the floor by the stove. "I suppose I'd better take Snowball out for a walk today," Mandie said. "He's going to get fat as a pig eating all that food you give him and no exercise."

"I hope you're not going to turn him loose and let him run back down to that house," Joe said. "Now that we know someone is in there it might be dangerous for Snowball to get too close to them."

"No, I intend on keeping him on his leash," Mandie replied. "I suppose I could walk him around the backyard after breakfast until it's time to meet the train."

"Do you mean you're not going to sit down there in the arbor and watch that old house before you meet Celia?" Joe asked.

"I could walk him down to the arbor as long as he is on his leash," Mandie replied.

"Just be sure you're back in time to go with me if you're going to meet Celia. And I would like to be a few minutes early at the depot just in case the train is a little early," John Shaw told her. "So we should leave about nine-thirty at the latest."

"All right, I'll wear my watch so I can keep up with the time," Mandie said.

"You don't have to," Joe said, pulling his pocket watch out to show her. "I always have mine with me. I had to get used to that at college to meet schedules."

Mandie glanced at the watch and said, "Oh, good, as long as you don't forget to wind it up."

At that moment the door opened, and Dr. Woodard came into the kitchen. "I smelled that coffee all the way upstairs," he said, smiling as he came to the table.

Aunt Lou brought a cup of coffee over to him as he sat down. He took a sip and told Aunt Lou, "That sure is good coffee. You made it just right."

Aunt Lou smiled at him and said, "But I didn't exactly make dat coffee, Doctuh. Mistuh John did 'fo I got in heah. He's a right good coffee maker."

"He sure is," Dr. Woodard agreed.

"Where are you going today, Doc?" John Shaw asked.

"I believe I'm just going to hang around here today," Dr. Woodard replied. "Since we're having all those folks in tonight I thought I'd just rest up."

"That's a right good idea. In fact, that's what I had planned to do," John Shaw said. "I have to go to the depot after breakfast and pick up the Hamiltons and then I thought I'd walk down to that old house on the creek and have a look around." He told the doctor about the information Mandie and Joe had given him and about the basket of food Aunt Lou had sent down there.

"Sure sounds like someone is staying there," Dr. Woodard agreed.

"I'd like to buy the property since those few acres join mine," John Shaw continued.

"And then will you tear down the house and build a new one, Uncle John?" Mandie asked.

"Well, I'd at least tear down the old one. It's about to fall in anyhow," John Shaw replied.

"But I wanted to give that property to Uncle Ned and build a new house on it for him and Morning Star to come live there," Mandie said.

"No, Uncle Ned would never leave his home at Deep Creek and come here to live," John Shaw said, and then, grinning at her, he added, "Maybe I'll just build a house on it for you when you get married."

Mandie felt her face turn red, and she wouldn't reply or look at Joe when he spoke up. "That would make a nice homeplace," he said.

Dr. Woodard looked at Joe and then at Mandie. "Now, I always thought Miss Amanda here would want to live in her father's house someday, over near our house," he said.

Mandie finally spoke. "Maybe I will someday."

Liza came in from the dining room and announced, "De table all set, Aunt Lou, and all de ladies be in de parlor."

John Shaw quickly stood up as Aunt Lou said, "Den we be ready for breakfast, Mistuh John."

"How about giving us time to go to the parlor and join the ladies, Aunt Lou?" John Shaw said.

"Sho' 'nuff will," the old woman replied.

Mandie and Joe followed John Shaw and Dr. Woodard to the parlor. Then Liza came to announce breakfast.

After the meal was over, Mandie and Joe took Snowball on his leash and walked down to the rose arbor. They sat and watched the old house for a while, but there was no sign of anyone down there.

Finally it was time to go to the depot. John Shaw drove the rig, and Dr. Woodard went along with them. Mandie was getting more excited about Celia arriving. She kept talking about what they would do while she visited.

"You'd think you hadn't seen Celia in a year, the way you're acting," Joe teased her. "What are you going to do when you are both grown up and go your separate ways?"

"Oh, we'll always live near each other, I'm sure," Mandie told him as John Shaw turned the corner.

"I wouldn't be so sure of that if I were you. You and Celia will both get married sooner or later, and who knows where her husband might want to live," Joe said.

Mandie grinned at him and teasingly said, "Oh, he'll live wherever she tells him they are going to live."

"Now, that won't work because he will have to have a livelihood of some kind, and that would probably determine where they live," Joe said.

"You are going to be a lawyer and you will be able to live wherever you want to, so maybe her future husband will be able to, too," Mandie replied.

"Now, Mandie, that's not exactly right. I'll have to live wherever I practice law, and not only that, I'll have to build up a clientele in one place and stay there," Joe replied.

John Shaw drew the rig up in front of the depot. Mandie glanced around. The train was not in yet.

"I'm going down to the platform so I can assist them with whatever hand luggage they have," John Shaw said, stepping down from the vehicle.

Mandie quickly followed him, and then Dr. Woodard and Joe joined them. She heard the train whistle in the distance and stopped to watch down the tracks. Trains always got her excited, and the fact that she could hardly wait to tell Celia about the old house built up that excitement still more.

At last the train came to a huffing, puffing stop by the platform, and Mandie could see her friend waiting in line to step down. Jane Hamilton and Aunt Rebecca paused to shake hands with John Shaw and Dr. Woodard, and Celia quickly scrambled around them and ran to hug Mandie.

"I'm so glad to see you," Celia said.

"I'm so glad you're here," Mandie added.

Then Celia saw Joe and rushed to hug him, much to Mandie's surprise. She noticed Joe's face turn red as he gently backed away.

"I haven't seen you in ages and ages, Joe. Mandie, please forgive me. I just got carried away," Celia told her.

"Just wait till you hear the latest about the mystery of the old house," Mandie replied.

Then Celia's mother, Jane, and Aunt Rebecca came to join them. They got in the rig while John Shaw and Dr. Woodard went to get their luggage that had been checked on the train.

"Oh, I have good news, Mandie," Celia said, glancing at her mother in the seat in front of them. "Mother says I can go with you to visit your Chero-kee kinpeople, provided we go when she isn't plan-ning for us to visit some of our relatives."

"Oh, I'm so glad, Celia," Mandie told her. "But when are you going to visit your relatives?"

Jane Hamilton turned halfway in the seat to look back at Mandie. "That is more or less flexible," she said. "I think we can work out dates with your mother about when y'all are going to visit your rela-tives."

"Joe is going, too," Mandie said, looking at him. "In fact, we're going to stay awhile at his house. Joe, when will you be out of school for the summer?"

"I'm not sure yet. It will depend on whether I want to take an extra subject next year, and if I do I'll have to take the examination for it, and that will be after the school formally closes for the summer. I'll know as soon as I get back to school," he said.

"And I'll have to talk to my mother and Uncle John about dates, too," Mandie said. "We can do that while y'all are here and get some ideas as to when we can all go."

"Are your mother and your uncle going with you, Amanda?" Jane Hamilton asked.

"I think Uncle John will go, but I don't know about Mother. We haven't discussed it yet," Mandie replied.

"I was hoping your mother would like to go to New York with me while you girls go visit your relatives," Jane Hamilton said.

"Maybe Mother might want to do that, but Uncle John has already told me he would like to visit our Cherokee kinpeople," Mandie explained. Then she had a sudden idea. "Why don't you take Grandmother with you? She likes to travel." She glanced at Joe, who grinned at her.

"Mrs. Taft? Well, of course she would be welcome to come along," Jane Hamilton replied. "Does she not have any plans yet for the summer?"

Mandie shrugged her shoulders and said, "She keeps telling me she wants to make some plans— plans that would include me—and I told her I wanted to visit my kinpeople, but you know my grandmother." She smiled at Mrs. Hamilton.

She smiled back and said, "In that case, maybe I can get her off your hands. I know she loves New York. Let's just keep this between us and I'll see what can be done." She winked at Mandie.

"Thanks," Mandie said with a big grin.

John Shaw and Dr. Woodard came back then, with the railroad helpers carrying the Hamiltons' trunks, which they put in the back of the rig.

"Looks like everything arrived all right," Aunt Rebecca said, watching the luggage. "We were so late checking things, I was afraid it would be delayed."

"I believe it's all there," Jane Hamilton agreed.

"Are you going to New York, too?" Mandie asked.

"I'm not sure yet," Aunt Rebecca replied. "I'm afraid I might not be able to handle Mollie in New York, and I haven't found a place to leave her yet."

"Will y'all be visiting the Guyers while you're in New York?" Joe asked.

"We will at least see them while we're there," Mrs. Hamilton replied.

"I thought maybe Jonathan Guyer might want to come down here and go with us to visit my Cherokee kinpeople, but I haven't asked him yet," Mandie said.

"I have an idea," Jane Hamilton said. "Why don't we arrange things so that y'all could go to New York with us and either go before or after that to visit your relatives?"

"We'll have to talk to my mother about that," Mandie said.

John Shaw and Dr. Woodard got in the rig, and as John picked up the reins, he said, "We're on our way now. I know y'all are tired after that train ride from Richmond."

"It's not really bad," Mrs. Hamilton said. "But I will be glad to get freshened up and get a cup of Aunt Lou's coffee."

"She'll have it waiting," John Shaw told her.

Mandie didn't want to say too much about the old house with the grown-ups around to hear, so she waited until they got to her house and she went upstairs with Celia to her room.

While Celia changed clothes, Mandie told her everything that had happened about the old house. "And now we know there is someone living in there because they took the food basket off the porch," Mandie concluded.

Celia quickly brushed her long auburn curls and straightened her skirt. "I don't know how you're ever going to find out who it is if they won't come to the door when you knock, and you said you watch and watch and no one ever comes out," she said.

"I suppose we have to keep watching and maybe we'll finally see someone," Mandie said.

"Anyway, come on, let's go. Joe is going to get tired of waiting for us downstairs."

Since the noon meal was not quite ready, Mandie and Joe took Celia down to the rose arbor and showed her the house.

"Somebody is living in that? Looks like it's going to fall flat any minute," Celia remarked.

"It's probably a tramp, or someone hiding from the law, or something like that," Joe said.

"Oh, goodness, and y'all have been going down there," Celia said with a loud gasp.

"But we haven't seen anyone so we don't know who is in there," Mandie added. "It could just be some poor person who doesn't have anywhere to live."

The day passed quickly. Before Mandie knew it, it was time to begin getting ready for the dinner party. Even though the house had plenty of guest rooms, Celia always shared Mandie's room when she came to visit. The girls discussed their dresses, and since Celia had brought a bright green silk dress with her to wear, Mandie put on her blue chiffon. They carefully arranged their hair, put on special jewelry, and even stole a whiff of perfume from Mandie's mother's atomizer.

When the guests arrived late that afternoon, the young people stayed in their own little group and observed.

"I'm glad Mother didn't invite anyone our ages that we would have to entertain, because after we eat we will be able to slip away and go watch the old house," Mandie said as the three stood in the parlor near the hall doorway, watching as the ladies and gentlemen came in.

"I believe there are ten people besides our own parents, so that is going to be quite a crowd at the dinner table," Joe remarked.

"Yes, but I'm glad because we won't have to carry on a conversation with any of them," Mandie said.

"And no young ones our ages that we have to be nice to," Celia added with a big smile.

"Oh, but look," Mandie said. "There is a little girl with the Harrisons."

Mandie and her friends watched as her mother greeted the Harrisons and then brought the little girl over to meet them. "Amanda, this is Mrs. Harrison's granddaughter, Cecily Millen." Elizabeth went back to her friends.

"Hello," Mandie said. The girl had brown hair, changeable eyes that flashed blue and green, and a tiny sprinkling of freckles on her nose.

"Hello," Cecily replied. She seemed shy without much to say.

"I'm glad you could come, Cecily," Mandie told her. "These are my friends, Celia Hamilton and Joe Woodard."

After Celia and Joe exchanged greetings with Cecily, Mandie said, "Would you like to go sit with us in the back parlor? The adults will be drifting in and out, but we could talk awhile before we go in to dinner."

"Oh, yes, that would be nice. Thank you," Cecily replied.

The four young people sat in the back parlor and got acquainted. Before they knew it, dinner was announced, and they were all seated together at the dining room table. Mandie liked Cecily and learned that the girl was eleven years old and was visiting her grandmother for the holidays. She lived in Tennessee.

Finally dinner was over. The guests began

leaving, and as soon as Cecily and her grandmother left, Mandie, Joe, and Celia went down to the rose arbor. The moon was not shining and the night seemed awfully dark, so when they sat down to watch the old house it was barely visible down the hill. But they also realized it would be hard for anyone down there to see them because of the dark night. They watched and watched with no results for what seemed like hours.

Finally Joe spoke. "Don't y'all think we ought to go back to the house now? The guests may be leaving and everyone will wonder where we are."

"I suppose we'll have to," Mandie agreed, standing up and smoothing her long skirt.

As she straightened up, something caught her eye down the hill. There was a faint light inside the old house. Her friends saw it at the same time.

"A light," Joe whispered.

"It's an awfully small light, whatever it is," Celia commented.

"And now that we see it, we're going to have to go back to the house. It's too late to stay here any longer. What luck," Mandie fussed.

"It wouldn't do us any good to stay and watch that light because we can't go down there and investigate. We are forbidden, remember?" Joe reminded her.

"I know, but sooner or later whoever is in there will have to come out, and I hope we see them when they do," Mandie replied.

The three slowly made their way back up the hill, stopping to look back now and then. The light stayed there and was visible in the dark night until they turned the curve at the top of the slope.

Once they were back in the yard of the Shaw house, Mandie stopped to say, "If we get up early enough in the morning we could go back and look before breakfast to see if the light is still there."

"Mandie, we'd have to come back before daylight in order to see the light," Joe reminded her.

"If the day is dark and cloudy like tonight has turned out to be, we could see it," Mandie replied.

"I hope it doesn't rain," Celia said.

"Yes, it would be too messy to go back in the rain like we did the other day," Mandie agreed. "But let's plan on meeting down in the kitchen real early tomorrow morning."

"If you insist," Joe finally agreed.

Mandie dreamed of the light that night, but she was as flustered in the dream as she had been earlier. She couldn't seem to get near enough to see anything. The light seemed to move farther away as she tried to approach it. Then she woke up in the middle of the night and couldn't go back to sleep for a long time thinking about it.

Chapter 11 / A Discovery

The next morning the three met in the kitchen, but to their dismay the weather outside was dark and cloudy with the threat of rain any minute. Joe built up the fire in the stove, and Mandie put on a pot of coffee, while Celia got down the cups and saucers.

By the time the coffee had perked, John Shaw joined them. And Aunt Lou came into the room shortly thereafter.

"Looks like it's going to be a rainy day," John Shaw remarked.

"Which means we're going to have to stay inside, I suppose," Mandie said in disappointment.

"That's right," John Shaw agreed with a smile. "I was hoping you would realize that. I don't want you going out in all this bad weather, Amanda. Even though we have a doctor with us, it would be terrible if you went out, caught a cold, and ended up spending your holidays moaning and groaning."

"Yes, sir," Mandie agreed.

"Has my father gone out this morning? Do you know?" Joe asked John Shaw.

"Yes, he went out about an hour ago, but he's only making calls in and around Franklin, so he'll be back for the noon meal," John Shaw said.

"After breakfast would y'all like to go to the back parlor and play checkers or something?" Mandie asked her friends.

"Fine," Joe agreed. "But there are three of us and we need a fourth person to even things up."

"I'll ask Aunt Rebecca if y'all want me to. She plays checkers with Mollie a lot," Celia offered.

Mandie and Joe both agreed. So that is the way they spent Saturday, because the rain never stopped and the wind outside was chilly.

At bedtime everyone hoped Sunday would be clear and sunshiny. They all planned to go to church in the morning and then the three young people would be free to watch the old house or whatever else they decided on.

During the night the wind woke Mandie. She raised up on her elbow to listen as it roared around the house. She could hear a loose shutter bang now and then, but there was no sound of anyone being up. Snowball had curled up next to her pillow, and Celia was sound asleep.

Mandie pulled the covers up around her shoulders and tried to shut out the sound, but it was almost daybreak before she finally dropped back off to sleep.

When daylight came, Mandie, Joe, and Celia went down to the kitchen. John Shaw and Dr. Woodard were already there and Aunt Lou was bustling around getting things ready for breakfast. The wind seemed to have subsided.

After everyone got coffee and sat down at the table, Mandie asked, "Did y'all hear the wind blowing last night? It woke me up."

Aunt Lou said across the room, "It sho' woke up Liza, too. She came to my room all cryin' and scared, and I had to let her sleep wid me de rest of de night."

"Yes, it woke me up, too," John Shaw said.

"Seems to have blown itself out this morning," Dr. Woodard said, drinking his coffee.

"It's raining again, though," John Shaw added.

"Are we going to church?" Mandie asked, still worried about the weather.

"We'll see what the ladies think," John Shaw said. "If they think we should stay home, then we can have our little Bible study together in the parlor this morning."

Snowball had followed Mandie down to the kitchen and started meowing at Aunt Lou until she set a saucer down with food on it for him. Then he began eating like he was starved.

"Please, everybody, help me watch Snowball. I sure don't want him to get outside in all this rain," Mandie said.

"We keep him right heah in de kitchen, my chile," Aunt Lou promised. "He sho' don't need outside."

When all the others were up, and everyone had gathered around the table for breakfast, the decision was made that they would stay home and John Shaw would lead them in a Bible study in the parlor.

Aunt Lou, Liza, Abraham, and Jenny joined them. Mandie noticed Liza was still nervous about the weather. Every time a strong gust of wind rattled a shutter, Liza would almost hold her breath. She would frown and clench her fists. Mandie tried to talk to her but she was too distracted to listen.

"Liza, this house has been here for years and years and years. My great-grandparents lived here. It's a good, strong house and I don't think it's going to blow away," Mandie said calmly as she sat next to Liza.

"Dey's always a fust time," Liza said without looking at her.

Mandie was secretly afraid herself, but she didn't want Liza to know it. She and her friends just looked at one another and didn't discuss the storm.

Later, when everyone sat down for the noon meal, Mandie glanced out the window and noticed the wind had almost completely subsided. The day was still dark and drizzly, though, and she knew she and her friends would not be going outside today to look at the old house down by the creek.

Conversation had picked up as the weather became quieter, and the adults talked among themselves around the table. The young people listened to part of it and were unusually quiet.

"I hope the weather clears up," Mandie remarked as she ate the beans on her plate.

"Me too," Celia added, sipping her coffee.

"We can always play checkers again," Joe said with a grin.

"And let you keep on winning?" Mandie teased.

Suddenly Aunt Lou opened the door from the hallway, and Uncle Ned came rushing into the room, "Tunnel!" He was almost shouting. "Go to tunnel. Tornado coming this way. Now. Go to tunnel."

Everyone jumped up in shock, dropping silverware and almost turning over chairs.

"Uncle Ned! You're back!" John Shaw exclaimed. Then, looking around the room, he said, "Quick! Let's get in the tunnel. It's safe in there."

"Hurry! Hurry!" the old Indian kept repeating as he stood just inside the room.

John Shaw led the way and everyone quickly followed him. "This way," he was saying as all the servants came into the dining room and followed. Aunt Lou put an arm around Liza and led her with the others.

Mandie was halfway down the hallway when she suddenly remembered Snowball. In all the excitement, Joe and Celia quickly followed the adults, but Mandie dropped back to get the cat from the kitchen without the others noticing.

Pushing open the kitchen door, Mandie ran to the woodbox behind the stove. He was not there. She looked under everything, all around the room. Snowball was not there. Noticing the back door was slightly open, she gasped and said, "Oh no, Snowball! I hope you didn't go outside!"

Pushing open the door, she looked around the back porch. There was no sign of Snowball, but she noticed fresh wet paw tracks leading out into the yard. She ran on out and was almost blown down by the wind. Straining against it, she managed to look around the yard. No sign of Snowball.

Suddenly she faintly heard meows of distress nearby. She searched the bushes and yard. "Oh, Snowball, come here! Where are you? Come on, Snowball!" she called and called.

Then there was a loud, angry meow, and she glanced up into the tree near where she was standing. There he was, clinging to a limb, his white fur ruffled, and crying as he watched his mistress below.

"Snowball! Snowball! Come down here!" Mandie tried to call over the roar of the wind as she stared at the cat in the tree. She held to low branches to keep from being blown away.

Snowball just clung to the limb up there and refused to budge. Rushing around the tree, Mandie tried to decide whether she could climb up and reach him. There were several low limbs, but the wind was forcing them every which way. She knew she didn't have time to go back and get Joe or one of the men to climb the tree and rescue the cat. And she couldn't go back into the house without Snowball.

"Snowball!" she called up to him as she paused by the lowest limb. "Stay right there. I'm going to get you down." The wind was drowning out her words, but the cat was watching from above.

Jumping to catch hold of a limb, she tried to swing herself up on it. Snowball was on the next limb above and she could almost reach him. As she clung to the limb, the wind whirled her about. She managed to reach up over her head and felt Snowball's fur. She couldn't look up. The wind was too strong. Grasping for the cat, Mandie grabbed the limb he was sitting on. Then all of a sudden the limb broke. She and Snowball tumbled to the ground.

Grasping her cat, Mandie didn't take time to figure out whether she was hurt or not. She pulled up her long skirts with her free hand and raced back toward the house just as Joe was coming out the back door. "Mandie! Where have you been? Come on. We have to get in the tunnel," he called as he came to meet her. He put his arm around her shoulders and they pushed their way back toward the house. The wind was so strong they could only take half steps at a time. It was impossible to talk. They were both about to lose their breaths from the gusts, and the noise was so loud it was deafening.

Finally, at the back door, Mandie and Joe fell into the house, managing to slam the door behind them. Then they ran to catch up with the others in the tunnel her great-grandparents had built under the house to hide their Cherokee friends when the Cherokee people were forced to move out of North Carolina.

Rushing down the hallway to the door that led into the tunnel, Mandie and Joe suddenly ran into Uncle Ned and John Shaw coming back out.

"Amanda! Where have you been? Come on, immediately!" John Shaw told her, giving her a little push through the doorway.

"Papoose look for cat," Uncle Ned declared as he followed.

"Yes, Uncle Ned, I couldn't find him. He was up in a tree in the backyard," Mandie turned back to say.

Uncle Ned smiled at her and said, "Papoose always look after white cat."

When they got down into the tunnel with the others, Mandie explained what had happened. It was much quieter down there, and she was able to talk and be heard. "I couldn't go and leave Snowball somewhere," she said, still holding her cat in her arms. Snowball was clinging to her dress with his claws and was still frightened.

"I don't be knowin' how dat cat got out," Aunt Lou said, looking around at the group. "Somebody musta left dat back do' open, dat's whut happened."

No one answered. The sound of the wind was stronger, and everyone gathered by the lantern someone had lit while Uncle John led them in a prayer. "Dear Lord, we beseech you, spare us and our friends and neighbors. Please calm the storm," he began, with all the others uttering "amens" now and then.

Mandie, with her eyes tightly shut, held firmly to Snowball with one arm and Celia's hand with the other while Joe tried to embrace both girls to protect them.

Liza was crying and Aunt Lou hugged her tight. "Be all right soon, baby," she whispered.

Mandie said to her two friends, "Our verse. Let's say our verse." She opened her eyes to look at Celia, who was speechless with fright, and Joe, who was trying not to show that he was worried.

Both agreed with Mandie and together they recited Mandie's favorite Bible verse, " 'What time I am afraid I will put my trust in Thee.' "

Then, taking a deep breath, Mandie tried to smile at her friends as she said, "Now everything will be all right."

Celia and Joe only nodded.

And at that moment the noise of the wind suddenly subsided and the tunnel became quiet as all the others looked at one another.

"Passed," Uncle Ned determined.

"Yes, I believe it has passed," John Shaw agreed. "Shall we take a look?" He and Uncle Ned started for the door leading to the steps that went back up into the house.

"And I'll go with you," Dr. Woodard added.

Elizabeth looked at them and said, "Please be careful. There could be some damage to the house up there."

"Yes," Mrs. Taft agreed. "I've lived through one of these storms before and it can be devastating."

"So have I," Mrs. Woodard added.

Aunt Lou started to follow John and Ned. John turned back to say, "No, Aunt Lou, I want you to stay down here until we look things over. Everyone, please wait. We'll be back shortly."

Mandie watched as the men left the tunnel. She was hoping they wouldn't run into any damage and get injured. The way the wind had roared, it was impossible to know how much fury it had poured out on the house.

When everyone was beginning to get worried

about the men, they finally returned.

"No damage to the house that we can find, thank the Lord," John Shaw announced. "Some of the trees are down but luckily didn't hit anything."

"Then is it safe to go back upstairs?" Elizabeth asked as she stood up from the stone bench where she had been sitting with Mrs. Woodard and Mrs. Taft.

"Yes, I believe so," John Shaw replied. "Just be sure you look around you for any damage we didn't find. But I believe the house is safe."

Everyone followed the men back up the steps into the house. Mandie still held tightly to Snowball, who had not calmed down. Looking about as they went, Mandie noticed the kitchen table had moved . . . across the kitchen. In the dining room they found the food still on the table but in somewhat different places from where they had left their plates.

"Lawsy mercy," Aunt Lou said, looking at the dining table. "We sho' do need to eat some mo' of dat food 'fore it goes bad." Turning to Liza, who was clinging to her apron, she said, "Liza, git in de kitchen and git a fresh pot of coffee goin'." She removed Liza's hands.

Liza finally straightened up and said, "Yessum, Aunt Lou," and went out of the dining room.

Mandie hurried over to a window to look out where the shutter had been blown open. "Oh, what a mess!" she exclaimed, gazing at the tree limbs scattered all over the yard.

"Just be thankful we have a good strong house," John Shaw said, standing behind her.

"A good, strong house!" Mandie repeated in excitement. "Uncle John, did y'all check on that old house down by the creek? It's not strong."

John Shaw straightened up, looked at Uncle Ned, and said, "I believe we'd better take a look down the hill. Of course that old house is in a gap and protected by the slope, but it could be damaged and someone could have been in it."

"Yes," the old Indian agreed.

"I want to go with you," Mandie said, quickly depositing Snowball in the woodbox behind the stove. "Aunt Lou, please don't let Snowball out."

Joe and Celia joined her as she followed the men out the back door. The wind had calmed and the sun was trying to peek through the stormy clouds that were sailing away into the distant horizon.

As soon as they reached the rose arbor, Mandie could see the place where the old house had been. It was completely destroyed. Pieces of lumber were scattered through the trees and countryside.

"Oh!" Mandie exclaimed as the three rushed on down behind the men. "I hope no one was inside that house."

When they got to the bottom of the hill, John Shaw and Ned began searching the area. The young people did their own searching, rushing about and looking under pieces of timber.

Then suddenly Mandie spotted something in a ditch down the creek. "Look!" she told her friends as she pointed and kept going. "Is that someone in the ditch?"

The men heard her and ran after them, but Mandie got there first.

Crouching there in a ball was someone who looked like a young boy. He wasn't moving.

Mandie put her hand on the boy's shoulder and asked, "Are you all right?" There was no movement or response.

Then John and Uncle Ned took charge.

"Thank the Lord Dr. Woodard is at the house," John Shaw said as he tried to rouse the boy.

"Hurt," Uncle Ned said. Stooping down, he picked up the boy and said, "We go house. Doctor see."

"Yes, yes," Mandie excitedly said.

They all followed the old Indian back up the hill as he carried the boy, who seemed to be unconscious. They entered through the back door, and Uncle Ned laid the boy on a cot at the end of the kitchen.

Mandie stood by watching, and when Uncle Ned stepped back, she said excitedly, "That's not a boy! It's a girl! Look!" She pointed to the long, dark hair where the cap had fallen off.

Dr. Woodard came hurrying into the room. "All right, let's clear some space here," he said, reaching for the girl's hand to feel for a pulse.

As everyone stood back and waited, Dr. Woodard examined the girl and said, "She's breathing but she seems to be in shock. John, we need to get her in a warm bed with some hot water bottles."

Aunt Lou took charge then. "I turn down de kivvers in dat fust room on de right upstairs. Liza, you start fillin' some water bottles." She hurried out of the room.

"A girl!" Mandie exclaimed. Turning to her friends, she said, "Do y'all suppose she has been staying all alone in that old house?"

"Yes, and I wonder what she was doing there," Joe replied.

"How awful! A girl all alone in that old house!" Celia exclaimed.

"I can't wait to ask her questions when she wakes up," Mandie told them.

Dr. Woodard heard her and turned to say, "No

questions anytime soon. This girl is in bad shape."

Mandie felt a stab of pain in sympathy for the girl. Here she was all alone and so ill she didn't know where she was. What would happen when the girl finally woke up? Would she talk and tell them anything?

And how could they help her? She must be in deep trouble, staying down in that old house all alone. Who was she? How did she get there?

So many questions. Mandie silently prayed for the girl to recover, but Dr. Woodard had said she was in bad shape.

Mandie remembered being all alone herself when she had run away after her father had died and she was sent to live with strangers. She was going to help this girl in every way she could.

Chapter 12 / Decisions

The girl was moved to the bedroom upstairs and still did not awaken. Dr. Woodard asked Aunt Lou if someone could stay with her just in case she became conscious.

"Why, sho', Doctuh, Liza kin stay wid dat girl," the woman replied as they all stood about in the hallway outside the room.

Liza quickly said, "But, Aunt Lou, I'se got work to do in de kitchen."

"But this is mo' important, Liza," Aunt Lou replied. "Now I—"

Mandie quickly interrupted, "Please, Aunt Lou, I want to stay with her. After all, Joe and Celia and I have been trying to find out who was down in that old house all this time. So I think it's our responsibility to stay with her." She glanced at her mother and Uncle John, who were nearby.

Aunt Lou also looked at Elizabeth and John and waited for them to reply.

"All right, Amanda, but we have other things that have to be done," Elizabeth agreed.

"And the menfolk will be outside cleaning up limbs and debris from the storm," John Shaw added.

"Then may I be first to stay?" Mandie asked hopefully.

"Yes, I suppose so, but we will all come up here from time to time to check on the girl," Elizabeth agreed.

"And the minute she opens her eyes I want to know. You come and get me," Dr. Woodard said to Joe. "I'll be outside with the men."

"Yes, sir," Joe replied. "But I could also come and help outside."

"No, I think perhaps you may be needed in the house to right some things that have been disarrayed by the storm," Dr. Woodard replied.

"Yes, sir," Joe agreed. Then, looking at Elizabeth, he said, "Mrs. Shaw, what can I do to help you in the house?"

"Nothing at the moment, Joe," Elizabeth replied. "If I find something that is too heavy for us women to handle, I'll let you know."

Dr. Woodard started to follow John Shaw and Uncle Ned down the hallway and called back, "Remember, only one person in the room at one time."

"Now we goes to see about dat meal we left on de table," Aunt Lou announced as she and Liza walked toward the staircase.

"And I'll check the contents of each room downstairs first to see if anything needs to be rearranged," Elizabeth said, following them. Mrs. Woodard, Mrs. Taft, and Jane Hamilton also went to help.

Celia moved over to sit on the bench in the hallway outside the door of the sick girl's room. Joe joined her, and Mandie stepped inside the bedroom.

The three young people took turns staying in the room with the girl for the rest of the afternoon. She didn't move, but Mandie thought her breathing sounded normal after a while. They discussed the girl and imagined all kinds of things about her.

"I wonder why she was dressed like a boy," Mandie pondered as the three sat on the bench, the nearby door propped open so they could watch for the girl to awaken.

"Maybe she ran away from home," Joe suggested.

"But if she ran away from home, why didn't she keep running instead of holing up in that old house? Your uncle John says she's been there a long time, according to the light he's been seeing," Celia said, looking at Mandie.

"Maybe she got lost, or tired, or something, and thought she ought to take time to figure out where she was going," Mandie replied. "Oh, I'll be so glad when she wakes up and we can talk to her."

"I just hope she isn't badly injured or ill," Joe said.

Mrs. Taft came down the hallway after a long time and stopped to speak to the young people. "Is she still asleep?" she asked.

"Yes, ma'am," the three chorused.

Looking at Mandie, Mrs. Taft said, "We need to discuss our plans for the summer sometime today so we'll have time to make arrangements."

Mandie's heart flopped as she replied, "Yes, Grandmother, whenever you say."

"I'll find out when it will be convenient to get together with your mother and your uncle," Mrs. Taft said. Then, glancing in the open door to the bedroom as she started down the hallway, she added, "I do hope that poor girl is going to be all right." And she continued toward the stairs.

"Oh, I dread this planning business," Mandie said with a loud puff of breath as soon as her grandmother was out of sight. Then, looking into the bedroom, she was startled to see the girl suddenly sit up and rub her eyes.

"Where am I?" the girl asked in fright as she looked around the beautiful, expensively furnished room.

All three of the young people rushed into the room. The girl pulled back under the covers as she stared at them.

"We're your friends," Mandie quickly told her. "You don't have to be afraid of us. We found you in the ditch where the tornado had blown that old house away. Are you all right?"

"Oh!" the girl exclaimed, her eyes filled with terror. "I remember. I thought I died but I must still be alive."

"Oh, you're alive all right and we're glad you made it," Joe said.

The girl looked around at the three and then asked, "Who are you? Where am I?" She still huddled under the covers.

"You're in the big house up the hill from the old house where you've been staying," Celia told her.

"Why were you staying in that old house?" Mandie asked.

"Oh, my things! Everything blew away! I have to go find my belongings," she replied, swinging her legs off the side of the bed.

"Wait, we'll help you, but first we have to let Dr. Woodard know you are awake," Mandie told her.

The girl paused to look at the group. "Dr. Woodard? Has there been a doctor here?" she asked.

"Yes, my father, and you just wait a minute now while I run and get him," Joe replied, hastily leaving the room.

"But I don't want a doctor. I'm all right. I have to find my things," the girl insisted.

Mandie held the covers as the girl tried to get out of the bed. "Please wait," she said. "Dr. Woodard is a friend of our family and just happened to be visiting here when the storm came. He asked us to get him when you woke up."

"But I have to find my things. Everything I own in this world was in a bag in that house," the girl insisted, reluctantly leaning back on the pillow.

"What is your name?" Mandie asked with a smile.

"Frances Faye," the girl replied.

"Frances Faye? What's your last name?" Mandie wanted to know.

"Where are you from?" Celia put in.

The girl looked at them both and finally said, "I suppose it doesn't matter anymore. You see, I was trying to keep anyone from seeing me and I kept thinking I should be traveling on, but I was tired and I got blisters on my feet and was waiting for them to heal. But then I got hungry because I ran out of the biscuits and meat I had brought with me. And suddenly I found a basket of food someone put on the porch. I ate a lot of it and decided to keep the rest for the next day. Well, the rats got to it that night and I had to throw it out." Her voice trembled as tears came into her dark brown eyes. "And I let your white cat come inside to catch the rat, which he did, thank goodness."

"So that's where Snowball was when we couldn't find him," Mandie said. "We'll get Aunt Lou—she's our housekeeper—to fix you something to eat."

Joe came hurrying back ahead of his father. Dr. Woodard smiled as he looked at the girl and said, "Well, now, I'm so glad you are feeling better. Do you have any aches or pain anywhere?"

The girl shook her head as she looked at the doctor and then put her hand on her stomach and said, "Just a little pain here."

"Because she's hungry, Dr. Woodard," Mandie told him.

"Well, if that's all that's wrong with you, we can fix that right quick, young lady," Dr. Woodard said, still smiling at the girl. Turning to Joe, he said, "Joe, pass the word to Aunt Lou that this girl is hungry and see what she can come up with."

"Yes, sir," Joe replied and hurried back down the hall.

Dr. Woodard sat down on the foot of the bed and said, "Now, tell me, why would a pretty girl like you want to put on boy's clothes?"

The girl frowned and finally said, "So people would think I was a boy and I'd be safer to travel."

"Safer to travel? Now, where might I ask were you traveling to?" the doctor asked.

There was a moment of silence before the girl sighed and then answered, "To my grandmother's house."

"And just where does your grandmother live?" the doctor asked.

The girl didn't reply and Celia spoke up, "Are you from Virginia? You say house just like I do—hoose—like all real Virginians speak. I'm from the country, just outside Richmond."

The girl quickly sat forward and said, "Richmond? That's where my grandmother lives—I think."

"You mean you don't know?" Mandie asked. "How can you go to her house if you don't know where she lives?"

The girl started crying and tried to hide her face behind her hands.

"I'm sorry. I didn't mean to upset you," Mandie quickly told her. Turning to Dr. Woodard, Mandie said, "She told us her name is Frances Faye."

"Frances Faye. Now, that's a right nice name, but how about the last name? Everybody has to have a last name," Dr. Woodard told her as he reached to hold her hand.

Frances Faye was so overcome she practically fell into Dr. Woodard's arms. He hugged her tightly and brushed back her long, dark hair. "There, now, let's talk about this. You can't talk and cry at the same time, can you? We are all ready to help you, but you must give us enough information for us to know what we can do." He continued stroking her hair.

Aunt Lou herself brought the food. She stood there in the doorway with a tray in her hands. Then, coming toward the bed, she set the tray down and said, "Lawsy mercy, this chile got to eat something right away, Doctuh. I believe dat cryin' spell is due to hunger, and we'se gwine fix dat right now." She plumped up the pillow behind the girl and straightened the covers as Dr. Woodard continued holding her.

Joe stood in the doorway watching. Mandie looked at him and shook her head. This poor girl seemed to be in bad shape, hungry and crying.

"Now, you jes' sit right back agin' dat pillow so's I kin put dis heah tray on de bed fo' you." Then looking at the three young people, she added, "Y'all jes' go sit in de hallway till dis heah chile eat. Den she'll feel mo' like talkin'."

"Yes, ma'am," the three chorused as they reluctantly left the room and went to sit on the bench in the hallway.

"She said her grandmother lives in Richmond," Mandie reminded Celia. "Maybe your mother knows her."

"Oh, Mandie, Richmond is a little bigger than

Franklin. We don't know everybody in town," Celia said. "The grandmother might be someone my mother knows or has heard of. We'll find out."

Mandie explained to Joe what the girl had told them while he was gone to the kitchen.

"But is she traveling on foot all the way to Richmond?" Joe asked in surprise. "I wonder where she came from?"

When Dr. Woodard told them they could come back into the room, they found the girl had been sitting at the side table in a chair and eating while Aunt Lou stood by encouraging her to finish the food.

Frances Faye looked at the young people as they stood around the room and said, "Thank you all from the bottom of my heart. I feel so much better now."

"That's good, because now we need to make a decision about some things," Dr. Woodard told her. "First of all, we need your last name and we need to know whether you are running away from home, or what?"

Mandie thought the girl was going to cry again, but instead she breathed deeply a few times and replied, "My name is Frances Faye Fordham and I am not exactly running away from home because . . . because . . ." her voice faltered for a moment, "because I don't have a home anymore. My mother died." She bit her lip and bowed her head.

Mandie rushed to her side to hold her hand and told her, "I understand how you feel, Frances Faye. My father died a while back and I was sent out to live with strangers to work for them tending their baby, and they were mean to me, so I ran away and came here to my uncle's house." She talked fast as she relived the memories in her mind.

Frances Faye looked at her and said, "My

mother was the only living relative I have, except for my grandmother and I've never seen her. She's my father's mother, and he died when I was a baby. We were living in Tennessee and I don't remember this grandmother ever coming to visit us."

"If your grandmother lives in Virginia we'll help you find her," Celia said. "My mother will know how to do that."

"My mother never would talk about my grandmother, for some reason," Frances Faye said. "All I know is she lives in Richmond and I suppose her name would be Fordham, like mine, since my father was her son."

Aunt Lou had been stacking up the empty dishes on the tray and now she looked at Mandie and said, "My chile, dis heah young lady be 'bout de same size as you. Why don't you find her a nice dress to put on so she kin come down to suppuh tonight?" She started out the door with the tray.

"Oh, of course, Aunt Lou," Mandie said with a big smile. "That's a good idea. Frances Faye, come with me to my room and pick out whatever dress you want to put on."

Frances Faye looked down at her soiled clothes and said, "But I have to go find my things that blew away."

"De men dun found dem things, but dey all wet, so we gwine wash everything," Aunt Lou explained and left the room.

Frances Faye looked at the doctor and asked, "Y'all found my things?"

"Sure did, but I hate to tell you everything was soiled because the bag was blown into the creek," Dr. Woodard explained. Then he smiled and said, "But I'm sure everything will be fine when they are washed."

"Oh, thank you," Frances Faye said.

The three girls went to Mandie's room, and Frances Faye was speechless with wonder as she surveyed Mandie's wardrobe full of beautiful dresses.

"All these are yours?" she asked.

"Yes, all of them, and you just pick out what you want to put on and you can have it," Mandie told her.

"But I couldn't take your clothes," Frances Faye said, looking through the garments.

"Remember what Aunt Lou said. You have to put on a dress in order to come downstairs for supper," Mandie reminded her.

"Well, I suppose I could borrow one," Frances Faye finally said. "But you decide which one."

Mandie flipped through the hanging garments and pulled down a peach-colored voile dress as she said, "Try this one. I believe you're just a little bit taller than I am, and this one is a little long on me so it ought to just fit you." She held it out to the girl.

"Oh, how beautiful! I've never had such pretty clothes," Frances Faye said, holding the dress. "Are you sure you don't mind if I put this on?"

"I don't mind at all, and I'm giving it to you if it fits, so let's find out about that," Mandie told her.

"You're welcome to use my brush and comb and hair ribbons," Celia said, pointing to the things on the bureau.

"Oh, we forgot something," Mandie said and hurried to open a bureau drawer. She started pulling out underwear. "You'll need these, too." She handed the girl a petticoat and other undergarments. "I believe they'll fit all right."

Frances Faye took the garments, and Mandie showed her the bathroom. "Just go in there and get dressed. We'll wait for you out here," she said.

Mandie and Celia silently waited in the armchairs until Frances Faye got dressed. When she came back into the room, Mandie smiled and stood up. "Well, no one would ever mistake you for a boy in those clothes."

Frances Faye smiled back and said, "I thank you so much."

"Let's go down to the parlor," Celia suggested.

"Yes, I know everyone else is waiting to meet you," Mandie told the girl.

When the girls entered the parlor, everyone in the room paused in their conversation to look at Frances Faye. Mandie's mother, Elizabeth, quickly stood up and said, "Come on in, Frances Faye, and meet everyone."

Introductions went around the room as Frances Faye shyly replied to each one.

After everyone settled back down, Jane Hamilton, Celia's mother, spoke to the girl. "I was told you are trying to get to Richmond," she said. "Celia and her aunt Rebecca and I will be returning to Richmond on the train at the end of next week and we would be glad to have you come with us. Maybe we can help find your grandmother there."

"Oh, thank you, Mrs. Hamilton," Frances Faye replied. "But I don't have any money for the train. You see, I've been walking from Tennessee."

"Never mind the money. We'll see to that," Jane Hamilton said. "We just want to help you out a little."

"Maybe my grandmother can repay you—that is, if I can find her," Frances Faye said.

"Don't worry about the money," Jane Hamilton said. "Just plan on going with us."

"Thank you," Frances Faye replied, almost in tears.

"We all want to help," Elizabeth said. "So plan on staying right here with us until it's time to leave on the train next weekend."

"I'm just speechless with thanks," Frances Faye finally managed to say without bursting into tears.

"Yes, dear, we all want to do something to help you," Mrs. Taft said. "Perhaps you will be able to come with us on our vacation this summer."

Mandie breathed deeply, getting ready for the argument she was sure would follow with her grandmother. *Might as well get it over with,* she thought.

"On your vacation?" Frances Faye asked. "But where are y'all going on your vacation?"

No one spoke for a moment. Then Mrs. Taft cleared her throat, looked directly at Mandie, and smiled as she said, "I don't really know where we are going. Amanda will have to tell us."

Mandie couldn't believe her ears. Grandmother was giving in to her wishes.

Mrs. Taft continued, "Amanda, what are your plans for the summer? Please tell us so we'll know where we are going."

Mandie grinned at Uncle John and said, "Well, it's like this. I don't really know, either. I want to visit my Cherokee kinpeople and maybe go to New York with the Hamiltons, and then maybe visit the Pattons down at Charleston with my mother, and maybe even visit New Orleans to see Joe's school."

Everyone was laughing as she finished.

"That sounds like a whole summer of traveling," John Shaw told her.

"It probably is, but since I knew everyone would not agree to everything, I just added it all together and whoever wants to can go wherever they want," Mandie said, grinning as she looked around the room.

All the adults began talking at once as they discussed the various places Mandie had mentioned. Mandie sat with her friends and didn't say another word. She had won this time. She would be able to go wherever she wanted to go without Grandmother supervising everything.

"We really would like for you to go with us wherever we do go," Mandie told Frances Faye. "And besides all those places, we could come to Richmond and visit you at your grandmother's."

"I sure hope I can find her," the girl said.

"Don't worry. We'll find her," Mandie assured her.

Mandie thought about her spring holidays, which would be over soon. She had spent the time well. The mystery of the old house was solved, and she had found a new friend. And now she had been given free choice of vacation.

There was also the mystery of the quilt with the Cherokee writing on it that she and her friends had found in the attic during the previous Christmas holidays. Uncle Ned had taken it to Uncle Wirt to decipher, and now she would be seeing Uncle Wirt this summer and could solve that mystery.

Things were looking up.

———

COMING NEXT!

MANDIE AND THE QUILT MYSTERY
(Mandie Book/36)

What does the Cherokee writing on the quilt say?